# What would *you* do if you found out ?

As ingers against the bottom of his eyes. Suddenly he ran his fingertips to the sides of his head, grabbed his ears, and started peeling off his face!

I gasped. Fortunately, the horrible noises coming from the room drowned it out. I wanted to get up and run, but I was too terrified to move.

I started to shake instead. Whatever Mr. Smith was, I was pretty sure the face he was slowly uncovering wasn't anything that had been born on Earth!

# My Teacher Is an Alien

## Bruce Coville

Illustrated by
**Mike Wimmer**

SCHOLASTIC INC.

New York Toronto London Auckland Sydney
Mexico City New Delhi Hong Kong Buenos Aires

**To my sixth-grade teacher,
Florence Crandall,
who told me to write a story**

No part of this publication may be reproduced, stored in a retrieval system, or transmitted in any form or by any means, electronic, mechanical, photocopying, recording, or otherwise, without written permission of the publisher. For information regarding permission, write to Aladdin Paperbacks, Simon & Schuster Children's Publishing Division, 1230 Avenue of the Americas, New York, NY 10020.

ISBN 0-439-80590-2

Text copyright © 1989 by General Licensing Company, Inc.
All rights reserved. Published by Scholastic Inc., 557 Broadway, New York, NY 10012, by arrangement with Aladdin Paperbacks, Simon & Schuster Children's Publishing Division.
SCHOLASTIC and associated logos are trademarks and/or registered trademarks of Scholastic Inc.

12 11 10 9 8 7 6 5 4 3 2         5 6 7 8 9 10/0

Printed in the U.S.A.     40

First Scholastic printing, November 2005

Designed by Elizabeth Wen

Special thanks to Pat MacDonald, Leslie Mendelson, and Erin Mendelson.

# CHAPTER ONE

# Missing—
# One Sixth - Grade Teacher

"Hey, Geekoid!" yelled Duncan Dougal as he snatched Peter Thompson's book out of his hand. "Why do you read so much? Don't you know how to watch TV?"

Poor Peter. I could see that he wanted to grab the book back from Duncan. But I also knew that if he tried, Duncan would cream him.

Sometimes I wonder if Duncan's mother dropped him on his head when he was a baby. I mean, *something* must have made him decide to spend his life making other people miserable. Otherwise why would he spend so much of his time picking on a kid like Peter Thompson? Peter never bothers anyone. Heck, the only thing he really wants is to be left alone so he can read whatever book he has his nose stuck in at the moment.

That doesn't seem like too much to ask to me. But Duncan takes Peter's reading as a personal insult.

So here it was, the first day back from spring vacation—we hadn't even gone into the school yet—and I could tell by the look on Duncan Dougal's face that the spring fight season was about to begin.

I clutched my piccolo case to my chest and watched as Peter's pale face began to turn red. Peter blushed at almost anything. He was tall and thin and wore thick glasses. And he was the smartest person I had ever met—grown-ups included.

The problem was, it was all book smarts. Peter had absolutely no idea how to deal with a creep like Duncan. Actually, neither did I. If I did, I would have stopped him. But the one time I had tried to come between Duncan and Peter, I ended up with a black eye myself.

Duncan claimed it was an accident, of course. "Susan just jumped right in front of my fist," he said as if I was the one who had done something wrong. To tell you the truth, I think Duncan punched me on purpose. Most guys wouldn't hit a girl. But Duncan doesn't mind. It was his way of warning me to keep my nose out of his business.

As I watched Duncan squinting down at Peter, it occurred to me that sixth grade can be a dangerous place if you don't watch out.

Stacy Benoit was standing a few feet away from Peter, pressed against the school wall and looking nervous. Stacy is this incredibly good kid, who never gets in trouble ever. She hates fights even more than I do.

She had just started edging her way toward me when Duncan ran his foot through a puddle and splashed dirty water all over Peter's jeans.

"Cut it out, Duncan," said Peter.

"Cut it out, Duncan," mimicked Duncan in a whiny, singsong voice.

Anyone who knew Duncan could see he was gearing up for a fight. But it wasn't necessarily going to be with Peter, since Peter usually just took whatever Duncan dished out. I figured Duncan was using him as a warm-up. So I was a little surprised when he tossed Peter's book into the puddle.

Even Duncan should have known that was something you just don't do to Peter.

"Oops!" he said maliciously. "I *dropped* it."

I heard Stacy gasp as Peter launched himself off the wall and bashed his head into Duncan's stomach. Within seconds the two of them were rolling around on the ground.

"I hate it when this happens," said Stacy as the

boys surrounded Peter and Duncan in a shouting, cheering circle.

The fight hadn't gone on more than ten seconds when a tall blond man came pushing through the crowd. Without saying anything, he grabbed the two fighters and hauled them to their feet.

*Wow!* I thought when I saw him lift the two of them right off the ground. *That guy is really strong.*

"Stop!" he said. Then he gave them each a shake and set them back down on their feet.

"Peter started it," said Duncan.

He's such a creep he probably didn't even know he was lying.

Peter wiped the back of his hand across his mouth. "I did not," he said sullenly.

I could see that his hand was trembling.

"No more," said the tall man, as if he really didn't care who started it. "Do you understand?"

"Yes, sir," mumbled Peter. I wanted to shake him. He made it sound as if the whole thing had been his fault.

"Do you understand?" said the tall man again, looking directly at Duncan.

"Sure," said Duncan. "I got it."

"Good," said the tall man. Then he turned on his heel and marched back into the school.

Duncan made a face at the man's back, then wandered off to find someone else to pick on.

"Who was that?" asked Peter as I handed him his soggy book.

"Who knows? I never saw him before. He's probably a new sub. Come on—let's go inside."

Peter and I were usually the first ones into school—but not by much. Our whole class went in early. That's because our teacher, Ms. Marie Schwartz, was so totally great. The thing I liked best about having her was that she was the only teacher in Kennituck Falls Elementary who always did a play with her class. I've always wanted to be an actress when I grow up. But until sixth grade, I had never had a chance to find out what it was like to be onstage. The play would be our last major project, and we had planned to start rehearsals right after spring vacation.

Unfortunately, when we got to our room, Ms. Schwartz was nowhere to be seen. The tall blond man was standing beside her desk, talking to a short, red-faced man who had almost no hair—our school principal, Dr. Bleekman.

Where was Ms. Schwartz?

Peter and I went to our desks. I wasn't happy. I had a bad feeling about this whole thing.

"The sub is handsome," whispered Stacy, who had come in behind us.

"I suppose so," I said grudgingly. "Where do you suppose Ms. Schwartz is?"

Stacy shrugged. "Maybe she's sick. Or maybe her plane didn't make it back on time. That happened to my third grade teacher once."

I nodded. That was OK. It was disappointing to come back to someone besides Ms. Schwartz, but I could cope with it for a day or two.

The other kids came into the room. Because Dr. Bleekman was there, everyone was super quiet. The bell rang, and we took our places.

"Good morning, class," said Dr. Bleekman. "I want to introduce Mr. John Smith. Mr. Smith will be your teacher for the rest of the year."

The rest of the year! I couldn't believe my ears! *What happened to Ms. Schwartz?*

Without intending to, I asked the question out loud.

# CHAPTER TWO

# Note of Doom

Dr. Bleekman glared at me. "Susan, if you have something to say, I expect you to raise your hand."

*Well, ex-cuuuuse me!* I thought. But there was no sense in making things worse than they already were, so I raised my hand. When Dr. Bleekman pointed at me I said—as politely as I could—"What happened to Ms. Schwartz?"

"That is a private matter," replied Dr. Bleekman.

What was that supposed to mean? Was she pregnant? Did she have some horrible disease? Did she get fired? And *whatever* it was, why hadn't she warned us? Why hadn't she said goodbye?

Without thinking about what I was doing, I stood up and said, "I want to know where she is!"

Dr. Bleekman looked at me in surprise. His cheeks got redder. "Do you know the meaning of the word *private*, Miss Simmons?" he asked.

"Yes, sir," I said quietly and slipped back into my seat. While I sat there, fuming, Dr. Bleekman blathered on about how he expected us to behave for our new teacher. Then he turned us over to Mr. Smith and left the room.

As I watched him go, I wondered if Dr. Bleekman had secretly fired Ms. Schwartz. I had always suspected he didn't like her—mostly because she didn't do things "by the book." I had heard them arguing about it once when I came back to school to get some papers I had left behind.

"Ms. Schwartz, I must ask you to show more respect for the curriculum," Dr. Bleekman had been saying when I walked into the room.

Boy, did that set Ms. Schwartz off. "Can't you respect the fact that the kids are learning?" she asked angrily. She grabbed the sides of her head in frustration. Clumps of her frizzy black hair stuck out between her fingers. "Listen, Horace. The kids will get more out of six weeks of doing a play than six months of dittos and workbooks."

Suddenly I wondered if having Mr. Smith meant that we wouldn't be doing our play.

I began waving my hand in the air again.

"Yes, Miss Simmons?" asked Mr. Smith.

*Miss* Simmons again. Were we going to have to talk like that for the rest of the year?

"Are we still going to do our play?" I asked.

Mr. Smith lifted one blond eyebrow in astonishment. "Play?" he said. "Of course we're not going to do a play. We're here to work!"

I sank back into my seat. Sixth grade was going bad faster than a dead fish on a hot day.

I could hear the other kids start to murmur their protests. Mr. Smith slapped his ruler against his desk.

"Dr. Bleekman hired me to straighten this class out. I can see now that what he told me about you was correct. Things have gotten completely out of control in this room."

Actually, that was only half true. Our room wasn't out of control; it just wasn't under Dr. Bleekman's thumb. Since most of us had already spent five years in rooms where the teachers did things Dr. Bleekman's way, we knew very well what he wanted a room to be like.

No question about it: Ms. Schwartz's room didn't fit the bill. But as far as we were concerned, things were going just fine. And not just because we were having a good time. We were also *learning* more than we ever had before.

My father claimed we were learning and having a good time for the same reason—Ms. Schwartz knew how to make things interesting.

For example, on the first day of school Ms. Schwartz stood at the front of the room and held up the sixth grade reading book, *Rockets and Flags* (popularly known as *Rodents and Fleas*).

"This," she said, "is not a good book." She held it away from her with two fingers, like a soggy tissue, and dropped it into the bottom drawer of her desk. "I know a better one," she said. "In fact, I know hundreds." Then she pulled a huge cardboard box from under her desk and started passing around stacks of paperback novels for us to choose from.

We spent the rest of the year reading *real* books. Sometimes we all read the same one, sometimes we all read something different. I remember mornings when we spent the entire reading period arguing about what some character should have done. Kids who had never liked reading before were really getting into it.

Unfortunately, Mr. Smith didn't believe in that kind of thing. In fact, the first thing he did after taking attendance that morning was pass out copies of *Rockets and Flags.*

Ms. Schwartz always read out loud to us, sometimes twice a day. She read wonderful books like *The Hobbit* and *The Sword in the Stone.*

When someone asked Mr. Smith if he was going to read out loud, he gave him a funny look and said it was "a waste of time."

Well, you get the picture. Over the next few

weeks Mr. Smith straightened us out all right. But you know how boring a straight line is. We had no more surprises. We pretty much stopped laughing in school. Things weren't terrible—just awfully grim.

Even the playground wasn't so much fun as it had been. Oh, Mr. Smith did keep Duncan Dougal from beating kids up. But he almost went nuts the first time he caught one of us playing a radio. Radios and tape players were banned from the playground. Mr. Smith didn't just hate rock music; he hated all music! I could see him shiver every time I picked up my piccolo and left the room for my music lesson.

After the third week of this I said something about it to my music teacher, Mr. Bam-Boom Bamwick. (Actually, his first name is Milton. But everyone calls him Bam-Boom because of his preference for thundering marches.)

Mr. Bamwick sighed. "Susan, you have to understand that not everyone appreciates the finer things in life," he said.

I guess that was as much support as I could expect. You know how teachers stick together.

When I got back to the room that day, it was time for our math test. I finished the test early. I was still feeling cranky about Mr. Smith's reaction to my piccolo, so I decided to write a note about it to Stacy.

"Mr. Smith is a total creepazoid," I wrote. That felt so good I decided to keep going. "He has totally ruined this class. Our whole year has gone down the tubes. The man is a total philistine!"

*Philistine* was a word I had just learned from my father. It means someone who has no appreciation for art and beauty. I thought it was a neat word, and I was using it every chance I could get.

A few more sentences and I was really wound up. This note was turning into a humdinger! At the bottom I drew an extra-tall, extra-skinny Mr. Smith holding his ears while I played the piccolo.

It wasn't a very nice picture. But when I was all done I felt better. I slipped the note under my test and waited for a chance to pass it to Stacy. I began thinking about how she'd react to my picture. I imagined her laughing so hard she fell off her chair.

Unfortunately, while I was daydreaming, Mr. Smith started collecting our papers. By the time I saw him walking up my row, it was too late to move the note. As I watched in horror, he snatched up my test—and my note along with it.

A wave of terror washed over me. I watched Mr. Smith walk away with my nasty note.

I closed my eyes and swallowed.

I was doomed.

# CHAPTER THREE

# An Unearthly Noise

The only thing I could think about for the rest of the day was how I was going to get that note back!

When we went outside for recess, I pulled Stacy aside to tell her what had happened.

"What am I going to do?" I wailed.

"I don't know," she said. "But you'd better do something because if that note has my name on it, Mr. Smith will get mad at me, too."

"Maybe he won't see it," I said.

Stacy snorted. "Are you kidding? He's checked every single paper we ever handed in."

Stacy was right. She always was when it came to that kind of stuff.

Actually, the heavy-duty checking was probably the best thing about Mr. Smith: he always handed back our papers. Of course, they never had a note or comment on them, just lots of red circles around the mistakes and a grade at the top. I didn't mind that on math papers, but it really annoyed me when it came to my writing. When Ms. Schwartz marked our stories and essays, she had always penciled in comments that showed she was paying attention to our ideas.

When Mr. Smith handed back an essay, it looked as though he'd been sitting next to an ax murder while he was marking it. The man must have bought red pens by the case. But all he used them for was to circle missing commas and misspelled words. He treated our essays like spelling tests.

I ask you, what's the point of writing something if that's the only response you get?

Finally I decided to try to get back into the building to see if I could snatch my note while Mr. Smith was still outside. If it had been Ms. Schwartz, I would have just asked if I could go to the bathroom. But Mr. Smith didn't believe in letting you off the playground for such a frivolous reason. He said by the time you were in sixth grade, you should know enough to take care of things like that in advance. The first three days after Mr. Smith came we had a line of worried-looking kids standing at the door each time recess ended.

The second-best method for getting off the playground was getting sick.

"I'll see you inside," I said to Stacy. Then I clutched my stomach, squinched up my face, and staggered over to where Mr. Smith was standing.

Later, I remembered that he was looking straight at the sun. But right then I was too worried about the note to pay attention to the fact that what he was doing should have burned out his eyeballs.

"Unnnyh," I moaned, trying to sound pitiful.

Mr. Smith looked down at me. "Is something wrong, Miss Simmons?" he asked.

"I don't feel good," I said. "I want to see the nurse."

Mr. Smith hesitated, then looked at his watch. "It's time to go in now, anyway," he said. "Line up with the rest of us. You can see Mrs. Glacka after we get in."

Now what? If I claimed I was about to throw up, he'd probably let me go inside right away. But if he was bringing everyone else in anyway, I wouldn't have the time I needed to go through the papers and find the note.

"All right," I moaned, trying to sound pitiful. I hoped it would make him feel guilty. I almost wished I *was* going to throw up. I'd make sure to hit his shoes!

Of course, once we were inside, I had to go to the nurse's office—even though I actually felt perfectly fine. Mrs. Glacka told me to lie down. I wasn't surprised. That was her basic cure for everything. So I lay there, staring at the ceiling and worrying about that note.

Finally I decided to follow Mr. Smith home. Maybe I could find some way to get the note back before it was too late. I didn't have any big plan, mind you. I was just desperate.

I wasn't sure where Mr. Smith lived. But I figured it couldn't be too far, since he always walked to school. So after the last bell I hung around on the playground, waiting for Mr. Smith to come out of the building.

I was concentrating so hard I almost jumped out of my skin when Peter Thompson came up behind me and said, "Hey, Susan, what are you doing?"

"None of your business!" I hissed. "Leave me alone!"

Peter's skinny face kind of crumpled, and he looked like he was going to cry.

"Look," I said. "This is private, OK?"

"Sure," said Peter. "I won't bother you." He tucked his book under his arm and walked away, trying to whistle. It was a pretty pathetic sound. I thought about Peter and realized with a shock that I was probably the closest thing he had to a friend.

That made me kind of sad. Not that there's anything wrong with having me for a friend. But I've got a lot of friends, and I didn't really think of Peter as being one of them. I liked him all right. He just wasn't someone I spent much time with.

I wondered if there was anyone who did spend time with him.

My thoughts were interrupted when I saw Mr. Smith come out of the building. I waited for a minute or two, then began sneaking along behind him. I tried to stay a half a block or so away. Whenever I could, I ducked behind a tree or a bush so he wouldn't spot me. I probably looked pretty weird. But that's one nice thing about being a kid: you can get away with this kind of stuff.

Mr. Smith's home was farther away than I had expected. He lived at the edge of town, in an old white house with black shutters. The house was set way back from the street. A thick hedge completely surrounded the lot on which it stood.

I stood outside the hedge feeling stupid. What had I hoped to accomplish by following Mr. Smith?

But I was in luck. As I watched from a hole in the hedge, I saw Mr. Smith set his briefcase down on the porch and go inside. Since it was a warm afternoon, I figured he planned to get something to drink, then come back outside to sit on the porch and correct our papers.

This was my chance! I scooted through a hole in the hedge and onto the porch. I was working up the nerve to open the briefcase when I heard an unearthly howl. It sounded like someone was trying to put a cat in a blender.

Hot as it was, I felt my blood turn to ice. What was going on in there? Had someone attacked Mr. Smith? I wasn't crazy about the man, but I didn't want him to be tortured or anything, which is what this sounded like.

Should I run for help, or go inside?

But what kind of help could I get? All I could say was that I had heard a terrible noise. Nobody was yelling for help, or anything like that.

I didn't think I could get anyone to come.

Then it occurred to me that maybe Mr. Smith really was putting a cat in a blender, or something awful like that. If so, he certainly shouldn't be teaching our class.

I decided to find out.

## CHAPTER FOUR

# Broxholm

The door was unlocked. Trying not to make any noise, I turned the knob and pushed.

The door opened without a sound. I hesitated for just a moment, then stepped in.

I was standing in a hallway. To my left I saw an empty living room—and I do mean empty. Except for curtains, there wasn't one bit of furniture or decoration in the room. The walls and floor were totally bare.

I flinched as another burst of horrible squawking and growling sounded above me.

Taking a deep breath, I began to tiptoe up the stairs. I was glad I was wearing sneakers.

About halfway up I stopped and thought, *What am I doing! I should get out of here while I can!*

You may not believe this, but the only reason I didn't turn back was that I thought Mr. Smith might really be in trouble. Even though I didn't like the man, I didn't want anything horrible to happen to him.

So I swallowed and took another step.

The noise stopped. Was everything over? Would Mr. Smith start down the stairs and find me standing here? I was just about to turn and run when another round of squawking and shrieking made it clear that whatever was happening was still going on.

I still *wanted* to run, but I was afraid to—afraid that if I did, I might read in the paper the next day that something terrible had happened to Mr. Smith. Something I could have prevented. Of course, I was afraid to keep going, but I decided I didn't have any choice. I took another step and then another. I held on to the railing as if it was a life line. The knot in my stomach got tighter with every step I took.

When I got near the top, I lay down on my stomach. I had read somewhere that when you're peering around a corner, you're less likely to be seen if your head is low. So I kept my head as low as possible. If I could have pulled out one eye and just stuck it around the corner to take a peek, that would have been fine with me.

The hall was as empty as the living room: no pictures on the walls, no rug on the floor. Through an open door at the end of the hall I could see a small, blue bathroom.

Closer to me, on the right, was another open door. The horrible sound seemed to be coming from there.

I decided low was the way to go. Still on my belly, I slithered down one side of the hall until I had reached the doorway.

I shivered. That noise was like a tiger running its claws down a blackboard; it felt like aluminum foil against my teeth. What could be making it?

When I finally got up the nerve to sneak a look around the bottom edge of the door, I saw Mr. Smith sitting at a little makeup table, looking in a mirror. Stacy was right. The man really was handsome. He had a long, lean face with a square jaw, a straight nose, and cheekbones to die for.

Only it was a fake. As I watched, Mr. Smith pressed his fingers against the bottom of his eyes. Suddenly he ran his fingertips to the sides of his head, grabbed his ears, and started peeling off his face!

I gasped. Fortunately, the horrible noises coming from the room drowned it out. I wanted to get up and run, but I was too terrified to move.

I started to shake instead. Whatever Mr. Smith was, I was pretty sure the face he was slowly uncovering wasn't anything that had been born on

earth! As he stripped away the mask I could see that he had skin the color of limes. His enormous orange eyes slanted up and away from his nose like a pair of butterfly wings. A series of muscular looking ridges stretched from his eyes down to his lipless mouth.

Soon the handsome face of "Mr. Smith" was lying on the dressing table. The creature that had been hidden underneath it began to massage his face—his real face. "Ahhh," he said. "What a relief!" He smiled at himself in the mirror, showing two rows of rounded purplish teeth.

I had noticed that the horrible noise was coming from a pair of flat pieces of plastic hanging on the wall. But it wasn't until Mr. Smith started "singing" along with the sound that I realized the plastic sheets were speakers. That hideous sound was music! Or at least what passed for music wherever my alien teacher had come from.

I was still trying to find the courage to start backing up when the alien turned down the music and flipped a switch on the table. The mirror began to shimmer. Suddenly the image of "Mr. Smith" was replaced by another alien face, this one just as horrible. Beyond the face I could see a big room, with other aliens bustling around. From the look of things, I figured this must be a spaceship.

The face in the mirror said something that

sounded like "Ign rrzznyx iggn gnrrr." The words were low and growly.

"Broxholm reporting," said Mr. Smith.

The face in the mirror made some growly noises.

"It is good to hear our mother tongue," said Mr. Smith—or Broxholm—or whatever his name was. "I cannot wait to return to the ship and have this language implant removed, so I can speak the true tongue, and not this barbaric garble."

*Hey!* I thought. *Whose language are you calling barbaric?*

But before I could get too angry, I heard something else—something that sent a cold chill down my spine.

"The testing process is proceeding on schedule," said Broxholm. "Before long I will have selected the students I wish to bring back for study."

Bring back for study?

I couldn't believe my ears. My teacher was an alien! Even worse, he had come to earth to kidnap kids and take them into space!

# CHAPTER FIVE

# How Strong Is
# an Alien's Nose?

The face on the screen smiled—at least, I think
it smiled. It's hard to tell with someone who looks
like that. Let's just say that all its teeth were
showing. Then it made a long speech in that awful
language. I felt like someone was grinding metal
next to my ear.

I don't know what he said. But it made Brox-
holm/Smith laugh. Well, I suppose it was a laugh.
His shoulders shook as if he was laughing. The
sound made my stomach turn.

When Broxholm stopped laughing, or whatever,
he reached down and turned off the screen. The
other alien faded from view.

Time for me to get out of there! I slithered back-
ward on my belly along the hall and then down
the stairs. When I heard the alien music come on
again, I relaxed a little.

On the porch I hesitated for a moment. Should I try to recover my note? A noise in the house made up my mind. Compared to what was behind me, any trouble I might get in because of that note was nothing. I jumped off the porch and ran all the way home, praying that Broxholm hadn't seen me.

Did you ever have something awful happen to you, and not really react to it until later? Like, you might almost get hit by a car on your way home from school, but not start shaking until after supper. It was like that with me that afternoon. It wasn't until I got home that what I had seen really began to sink in.

I ran up to my room, plowed my way through the mess, and collapsed on my bed. I lay there until supper, staring at the ceiling and shaking with fear. What was I going to do? What would *you* do, if you found out your teacher was an alien? Go to the principal? Tell your parents?

Think about it for a minute.

Imagine the conversation.

Not a pretty thought, is it?

The only person who might believe me was weird Peter Thompson. I decided to tell him what I had seen. If I couldn't convince him, I knew I didn't have a chance of convincing anyone.

I must have looked pretty bad when I went down to dinner because my mother asked me three times what was bothering me. But then, she tends to be a bit of a fusser. I try never to let her hear me sneeze, because if she does she decides I've got pneumonia and tries to pack me into bed for a week. All right, that's a slight exaggeration—but not much. She and my dad are always battling about how much freedom they should give me.

"Come on, Margaret," my dad will say. "She's in sixth grade now. You can't treat her like a baby anymore."

"Oh, Edward," my mother will reply, "you seem to think you can treat Susan the same way you would a boy."

Can you believe she actually says that?

Anyway, that night at supper she put her hand on my forehead and clucked about how pale I looked. I think she was actually disappointed that I didn't have a fever. At least then she would have known what to do.

"Are you still upset about Ms. Schwartz, Susan?" she asked, shoveling a load of broccoli onto my plate.

Actually, at the moment I was upset about the broccoli. But Ms. Schwartz was a close second. I nodded weakly.

"Well, I can tell you it wasn't Dr. Bleekman's fault," she said. "In fact, he's very upset that Ms. Schwartz didn't give him more notice. I talked to

Helen. She told me Ms. Schwartz didn't even have the courtesy to tell Dr. Bleekman face to face that she was leaving. He got a letter the first day of vacation, saying she wouldn't be back. That left him six days to find someone to take her place. I think he did very well to find that handsome Mr. Smith in such a short period of time."

"Mr. Smith is ruining our class," I said bleakly.

"Oh, don't be so dramatic, Susan," said Mom.

I'm planning to be an actress when I grow up. What should I be? Athletic? Besides, this so-called teacher was going to kidnap some of my classmates and drag them off to outer space. Suddenly I realized that I had been putting off the truth. He wasn't going to kidnap some of my class*mates.* If he was going to pick *someone* from my class, I might well be on his list. In fact, after he read that note, I might be his number-one prospect.

I swallowed hard. I was dying to tell my folks what I had learned, but I knew they wouldn't believe me.

That night I tried to call Peter. But I couldn't get any answer at his house. "Come on, Peter," I hissed at the phone. "Where are you? I need you!"

I let it ring fifteen times.

No answer.

I tried again an hour later.

No answer.

29

I was as nervous as a marshmallow at a bonfire.

It was even worse when I had to go to school the next morning. I didn't think Broxholm knew I had been in his house. But what if I had left behind some kind of clue? Or what if he had some kind of alien super-senses that would let him know I had been there? What about that weird, muscular nose? Just how powerful *was* his sense of smell? Would he know I had been snooping by my odor? I watched his nose carefully when I walked through the classroom door that morning. It didn't twitch or anything. But that didn't mean much. Maybe underneath that mask his real nose had sniffed me out. Maybe it was sending him a message even now. *There she is. That's the one who was in the house yesterday!*.

I sat down. I was so tense I felt as if I would explode if anyone so much as touched me. I wanted to pass Peter a note asking him to meet me on the playground at recess. But I was in enough trouble because of notes already.

We stood up and said the Pledge of Allegiance. Then Smith/Broxholm motioned me to his desk.

"I think you lost something yesterday," he said.

And then he handed me my note.

## CHAPTER SIX

# Drafting Peter

I sat at my desk and stared at the note. What was going on here? Was Broxholm playing with me?

For a moment the thought that he was actually being a nice guy crossed my mind. I brushed it away. Nice guys don't kidnap sixth graders and drag them into outer space. I decided it was more likely he was just sending me a message. *I've got your number, kid. Don't mess with me.*

I was so wrapped up in trying to figure out what was going on that I could barely concentrate on my work. Most of the time I just sat and stared at Broxholm's face, trying to figure out how the mask was attached.

When I started to wonder if there was any way I could pull it off, my imagination began cooking up a horrifying scene. In this daydream, I saw myself grab Broxholm's ears and begin pulling on them, trying to unmask him. Only the mask wouldn't come off. So I pulled harder. Suddenly his face began to stretch and twist all out of shape. But still the mask wouldn't come off.

It was gross.

*Stop it!* I told my brain firmly.

But the vision kept coming back.

Sometimes I wonder about my brain; I mean, it seems to have a mind of its own. If it was really *my* brain, you'd think I would have a little more control over it, wouldn't you?

When you get right down to it, brains are pretty weird.

But not as weird as having an alien for a teacher.

By the middle of the morning, I was beginning to wonder if this whole alien business had been a bad dream. It seemed too impossible to believe.

But I knew I hadn't been dreaming. It *was* real.

My teacher was an alien.

I couldn't wait to get Peter aside so I could talk to him.

When recess came, I tried to act calm as I wandered over to the wall where Peter usually sat to read. He was sitting on the ground, cross-legged, clutching a book called *A Princess of Mars* in his skinny hands.

I slid down the wall and sat beside him.

He acted as if he didn't notice me. Or maybe he really didn't. He was one of those kids who could get so wrapped up in a book it would take a bomb to break his attention.

I hated to interrupt him. Peter always seemed a little unhappy to me, like he understood that he just didn't fit in with the rest of us. The only thing I knew that made him happy was reading science fiction. He always had a book hidden behind his school book. The neat thing was, it didn't make any difference, because he was so bright that whenever the teacher asked him a question, he always knew the answer. I could never figure out why they wouldn't just leave him alone and let him read. But that's the way school is, I guess.

"So, what's going on?" I said.

What a stupid line ! I'm glad I'm a girl, because when I get older the *guys* are going to have to come up with lines when they want to start a conversation. Now there's one job I'll be glad to let them have!

Peter lifted his nose out of the book and looked at me as if *I* were the alien. He blinked, and I realized he was trying to come back to the real world. I felt bad for interrupting him. In class he had to read with one eye on the teacher. Out here he probably planned on shutting everything out for a while.

I hesitated for a minute. How was I going to say this?

Finally I just decided to jump right in. "I need your help," I said.

Peter looked surprised. "For what?" he asked.

I realized I hadn't jumped in after all. The biggie was still to come.

"Promise you won't laugh at me?" I asked.

Peter shrugged. "Sure, I promise."

"All right, listen. I know you're not going to believe this, but I found out something awful yesterday. Mr. Smith is an alien. He's come here to kidnap a bunch of kids and take them back to outer space."

I held my breath to see what Peter would say. I thought he might laugh, or tell me to get lost, or—and this thought really scared me—shout it out to everyone else. To my astonishment, he didn't do any of those things. He just looked as if he was going to cry.

"What's the matter?" I asked.

"You should know," he said. He sniffed and wiped the back of his hand across his nose.

What was going on here? I had a sudden thought that maybe he was an alien, too. That was stupid, of course. But I had aliens on the brain, and I couldn't figure out what else it might be.

"I *don't* know," I said. "Honest I don't."

He looked at me, and his eyes were so sad they made me want to cry, too.

"I always thought you were the one kid in this class who was on my side," he said. "Like that time you tried to stop Duncan when he was beating me up. I *expect* everyone else to tease me. I just never thought *you* would do it."

Now it was my turn to be mad. "I'm not teasing!" I yelled. Then I lowered my voice. "I'm not teasing!" I hissed. "I'm serious."

Peter stared at me. "Is this some kind of game?" he asked.

I hesitated. If I told him the truth, he probably wouldn't believe me. If I told him it was a game, he might at least help me think things through.

What a fix! The only way I could get him to believe me was to lie to him.

"Yeah," I said. "I thought you were the one guy in this class with enough imagination to play. But now you've ruined it."

"No!" said Peter. "No, we can still play. Just pretend you had to tell me it was a game to get me to believe you."

My head was starting to spin. Peter was using my reason for lying as a reason to pretend that what he believed was a game was for real. Or something like that. This was getting too complicated for me.

*This is going to be one of those weeks,* I thought. *The only person I can count on for help stopping an alien invasion thinks the whole thing is a game!*

Well, as my grandmother always says, you make do with what you've got.

And Peter was what I had. I decided to stop worrying about who was believing what and just tell him what had happened.

"Well?" I said when I was done. "What do you think we should do?"

Peter stared at the sky for a minute. He rubbed his chin as if he was thinking really hard.

Then he gave me his answer.

"We've got no choice," he said. "We'll have to break into Broxholm's house to look for evidence."

# CHAPTER SEVEN

# Night Expedition

Peter was right, of course. That was the worst thing about it.

And what did I say? Now that I had someone who was willing to help me and had actually given me some good advice, did I say, "Thank you very much?"

Are you kidding? I looked at him and said, "You have got to be out of your mind!"

"I am not!" said Peter indignantly. "If we're going to do anything about Broxholm we have to have proof. And the only way to get proof is to get into his house and find some."

I thought about that. I couldn't come up with any way around it. How else could we find proof that we were telling the truth?

Then I thought of something else. "I don't think it will do any good," I said. "There's not much in there. He doesn't have any furniture or anything."

"How do you know that?"

"I told you, I was in there yesterday."

"Oh, yeah," said Peter. "I forgot."

I could tell he still thought I was making this up.

"Did you see the whole place?" he asked.

I shook my head.

"Well, maybe there's something in his bedroom," he said. "Or the attic. Or the kitchen." His face lit up. "That's it!" he said. "The *kitchen*. Who knows what they eat on the planet he comes from? I bet we'll find all kinds of gross alien slime in his refrigerator!"

"Peter, you're brilliant!" I said. I was actually starting to feel hopeful. All we needed was just one thing that would prove I wasn't making all this up.

"Now, when can we do it?" I asked. "We can't let him catch us!"

Peter thought for a minute. "There's a PTA meeting tomorrow night," he said. "I heard Dr. Bleekman say that all the teachers have to be there. That's the only time we can be sure Broxholm will be out of his house.

"Tomorrow it is," I said.

That was Wednesday. By the time Thursday afternoon rolled around, I was a wreck. I had spent two full days sitting in that classroom, staring at

Mr. Smith and knowing his handsome face was only a mask—a mask that hid the terrifying face of an alien.

While none of the other kids were crazy about Mr. Smith, they didn't think there was anything really wrong with him. Only Peter knew the secret—and he thought it was a game I had invented.

"What about Dr. Bleekman?" he said to me during afternoon recess.

"What about him?" I asked.

"Do you think he's in cahoots with Broxholm? They seem pretty chummy."

I shook my head. "My mother told me Dr. Bleekman was really angry with Ms. Schwartz for quitting so suddenly. He wouldn't have been upset if he'd been wanting to put Broxholm in her place."

Peter looked at me in astonishment. "Don't you know a cover story when you hear one?" he asked. "Of course he acted like he was upset! If he hadn't, it would have been suspicious. The way I figure it, Broxholm asked Dr. Bleekman which teacher he wanted to get rid of the most. Then he zapped Ms. Schwartz so there would be a spot for him to fill."

I felt like there were ants crawling on my skin. Peter was just playing a game. But what he said made sense—too much sense. I still couldn't believe that Ms. Schwartz had just quit without saying anything to us. Something must have happened to her.

My head was whirling. Was Dr. Bleekman really in on the whole thing? Had Broxholm really fried Ms. Schwartz? If so, what would happen if he caught Peter and me in his house? If Broxholm found some way to get himself excused and came home early to catch us rummaging through his house would he zap us, too?

That last question really terrified me.

But if the ideas Peter was spinning out were true, it was more important than ever that we unmask Broxholm.

"How are you going to get out tonight?" I asked Peter.

"What do you mean?" he asked.

"What do you mean, what do I mean? How are you going to get out of your house tonight?"

I had no problem myself. My parents were officers in the PTA, and they *always* went to meetings. They had decided at the beginning of the year that I was too old for a baby-sitter, so as long as I was back before they got home, it wouldn't make any difference. I didn't really like sneaking out on them, but this was a matter of life and death.

Peter looked at me in surprise. "Are you really planning to break into Mr. Smith's house?" he asked.

"His name isn't Smith," I said. "It's Broxholm. And, yes, I'm really planning to *search* his house." (I couldn't bring myself to call it a break-in). "I have to have some way to prove what he really is."

Peter looked troubled. He rubbed his hands over his skinny face. Then he looked me straight in the eye and said, "This isn't a game, is it?"

I shook my head.

Peter's eyes got wide. He swallowed a couple of times. Then he took a deep breath and said, "Don't worry, I'll be there."

I could have hugged him.

That night I met Peter at eight o'clock on the corner of Pine and Main. He was carrying a flashlight, which made me feel stupid, since I had forgotten mine. It was nearly dark. The crickets were singing, and the moon had already risen. Even though it was May, it was cold. Or maybe I was just cold because I was scared.

"Ready?" I asked.

Peter nodded. "Ready," he said.

We each took a deep breath.

Then we set off for the alien's house.

"I was afraid you might not come," I said after we had gone a few blocks.

Peter shrugged. "I didn't want you doing this alone," he said. "For a while I was afraid you were trying to pull a joke on me. I thought when I got to the corner, you and some of the others might jump out and start laughing at me."

"Hey!" I said. "I wouldn't do something like that!"

"I didn't think so," said Peter. "That was one reason I came. The other reason was, I figured if you really *were* going to break into Mr. Smith's house, this must be for real. You're not the kind of kid who would do something like that unless it was serious."

"Believe me," I said, "this is serious."

"I believe you," he said nervously.

We didn't say anything else until we got to Broxholm's house.

"Well," said Peter. "Here we are."

"Here we are," I echoed.

But neither of us moved. We just stood there looking at the dark empty house. I don't know about Peter, but I was trying to talk myself into taking the next step. To tell the truth, I was so scared I thought I might wet my pants.

## CHAPTER EIGHT

# The Alien's Lair

I don't know how long we stood there, trying to build up enough courage to go in. I do remember looking up at the sky. It was as dark as black velvet, and the stars were like diamonds scattered across it.

*Which one of them did you come from, Broxholm?* I thought. *And why did you have to come here?*

I heard Peter sigh beside me. "Isn't it wonderful?" he asked, swinging his arm up and out to indicate the entire sky. "Don't you want to go there?"

"You've been reading too much science fiction," I said. "Come on—let's get this over with."

Sharp leaves scraped against our faces as we pushed our way through the hole in the hedge. On the other side we dropped to our hands and knees and crawled across the lawn. Even though we were pretty sure Broxholm wasn't home, we didn't want anyone else to see us and interrupt our mission. The lawn was drenched with dew. By the time we reached the porch the knees of my pants were soaked through and I was freezing.

"How are we going to get in?" whispered Peter.

Good question! It may sound stupid, but I had been so worried about *what* we were doing that I hadn't thought about *how* to do it.

"I don't know," I hissed back. "How do people usually break into places?"

Peter looked at me in disgust. "How would I know?" he asked. "I'm not a burglar."

"Well, neither am I!" I snapped.

I closed my eyes. Fighting wasn't going to get us anywhere. "Let's circle the house," I said. "Maybe we'll find an open window or something."

We crept along the side of the house. As Peter played his flashlight over the windows I felt thankful for the hedge that masked us from the street.

"Nothing on this side," he whispered.

"Check down low," I said. "Maybe one of the cellar windows is open."

But they were all sealed shut.

Peter gestured toward the back of the house.

Just around the back corner we found one of those slanting cellar doors. It was padlocked shut.

But the wood was half-rotted, and when Peter shook the lock, the whole thing came loose in his hand. He set it aside and carefully lifted the door. It creaked for an eternity as it came open. I found myself staring down into a well of perfect blackness.

"Dark," I whispered.

"Sure is," said Peter.

Then he took a step forward.

I followed him, wondering if Broxholm had booby-trapped the place. Then I wondered what kind of booby traps an alien would use: lasers that would cut us off at the knees? Stun guns? Freeze rays? Hey, these guys had come here from another star system. Who knew what they could do?

We walked down eight concrete steps. At the bottom we came to a wooden door so old it had a latch instead of a knob. Peter lifted the latch and pushed. Nothing. He put his shoulder against the door and shoved again. It swung open with an eerie creak.

"After you, madam," he whispered.

"Well, at least shine your flashlight in there," I hissed.

He pointed his beam through the door. I couldn't see anything special—just a dusty cellar, the kind you'd expect in an old house.

"Let's go together," I whispered.

Peter took pity on me, and we stepped through the door side by side.

"I don't think we're going to find anything down here," he said, shining his light around the cellar. I agreed. Except for the furnace, the stairs up to the first floor, and the cobwebs, the space was completely empty.

Without speaking, he headed for the stairway. I ran into a cobweb. I shivered when the wispy, clinging threads brushed over my forehead.

"You don't suppose Broxholm has any friends here, do you?" whispered Peter when we were about halfway up the stairs.

I stopped. "I don't think so," I said after a minute. "He didn't mention any when he was talking to the guy in the spaceship."

Peter nodded. But he had managed to make me even more nervous than I had been to begin with. What if there *was* another alien here? What would he do if he caught us snooping around?

"Where to?" asked Peter when we reached the top of the stairs.

"Let's try the kitchen," I said, remembering his idea about alien food.

But when we opened the refrigerator, all we saw were a bunch of cold cuts, a half-empty carton of milk, a bottle of catsup, and two six packs of beer.

"He sure doesn't eat like an alien," said Peter. "Are you sure this guy is from another planet?"

"Let's go upstairs," I said. "I'll show you the thing I saw him talking into."

Peter closed the refrigerator door. But before he would leave the room he insisted on checking the cupboards. He even opened the peanut butter jar to see if it really had peanut butter in it, and not some kind of extraterrestrial goo.

The second floor had three rooms. I had high hopes for the bathroom; I thought we might find some sort of weird shampoo there or something. But it was as disappointing as the kitchen. Even the medicine cabinet was filled with typical brand name items.

"Do you think Mr. Smith really uses Excedrin?" asked Peter. "Or is this just here to convince people he's a teacher?"

"If he was stocking his house to fool snoopers, he'd have put in some furniture," I said.

The only place where we found anything even remotely alien was the room where I had seen Broxholm talking to the man on the ship. The two speakers that looked like pieces of flat plastic were still hanging on the wall. I looked under the dressing table, and found the switch Broxholm had used to tune in his ship. I reached out to touch it, then pulled my hand back. What if I somehow turned it on and the man from the ship saw Peter and me standing there?

"Come on," said Peter. "We might as well go."

"You don't believe me anymore, do you?" I asked sadly.

Peter shrugged. "This place is kind of weird, what with no furniture and everything. But there's nothing that would make anyone think Mr. Smith is an alien. I believe that you believe what you told me. But whether it's true or not . . ." He shrugged and turned to leave the room.

"Wait," I said, following him into the hall. "We still didn't try that door."

Peter swung his flashlight in the direction I was pointing.

"It's just the attic," he said.

I knew that; I could tell by how narrow the door was. But that wasn't the point.

"So what if it's the attic?" I said. "Maybe Broxholm has something packed away up there. Come on, Peter. We've gone this far. We can't give up now."

"Oh, all right," said Peter. He opened the door and started up the stairway. When he got about halfway up the stairs his head passed the level of the attic floor. I was walking so close that I bumped into him when he stopped.

"What is it?" I whispered.

When he didn't answer me, I pushed my way up beside him and cried out in horror.

# CHAPTER NINE

# The Force Field
# in the Attic

For a long time neither of us said a word.

"Is she alive?" I asked at last.

Peter didn't answer me.

"Peter," I hissed, pinching his arm. "Do you think she's alive?"

Peter turned to me. I could see his face in the blue glow that came from the thing in the center of the attic. His eyes were glazed and blank. I wasn't sure whether he even knew I was there.

"Peter!" I hissed.

He shook his head. "You weren't kidding, were you?"

"Of course I wasn't kidding!"

"But do you know what this means?"

"Yeah. It means we're in big trouble. Now let's get up there and see if we can figure out what's going on."

"An alien!" said Peter, his voice filled with awe. "Mr. Smith is an alien! We're not alone!"

"What are you talking about?" I hissed.

"Intelligent aliens. Mankind is not alone in the universe."

"Well, I'm feeling pretty alone right now," I said. "Are you going to help me or not?"

Peter closed his eyes and rubbed his face. Suddenly his awe turned to fear. "Oh, my God," he said. "What if Mr. Smith catches us here?"

I rolled my eyes. "Why do you think I've been so scared all night, you yo-yo?"

Suddenly I realized what was going on. "You never did believe me, did you?" I said angrily. "You thought this was all just a joke!"

Peter shook his head. "I believed you," he said. "But I didn't really understand what it meant until—well, until I believed it this way." He shrugged helplessly. "I can't explain it," he said.

It didn't make any difference. I understood. He was feeling the way I felt when I saw Broxholm take his face off.

"Come on," I said. "Let's get up there."

Despite my brave words, I climbed the rest of those stairs pretty slowly. Peter climbed up beside me. Standing side by side, we stared at the terrible thing we had found.

In the center of the attic was a column of blue light. It was about three feet across, and stretched from the floor to the peak of the ceiling. And in the center of it stood—Ms. Schwartz. Her eyes were wide open, but they hadn't blinked once in all the time we had been looking at her. Her frizzy black hair was standing straight out from her head, as if she was getting some kind of horrible shock. Her hands were at her sides, palms forward, fingers separated.

I looked carefully, but I couldn't tell if she was breathing.

"Is she alive?" I asked again.

"I don't know," said Peter. "It's hard to tell."

We stepped forward. Ms. Schwartz didn't move. The air smelled funny. My hair started to move by itself. I could feel a strange tingling on my skin.

"It's a force field," said Peter, taking another step forward.

I *knew* he was the right person to bring with me. Only a person who read that much science fiction would know what to call something like this. Now if he only knew what to do about it!

Unfortunately, he didn't.

"If I could figure out where it came from, maybe I could turn it off," he told me. "But I don't see any equipment. Besides, I'd be afraid of hurting Ms. Schwartz."

I nodded. "Do you think she's OK in there?" I asked, blinking back a tear.

How had Broxholm done this to her?

Maybe the handsome creep had tricked her into going out on a date with him. What a treat—a date with an alien. I could just imagine his line: *Let's go see a film. Then I'll take you back to my house and lock you in a force field.*

What a rat!

"Oh, Ms. Schwartz," I moaned. "What are we going to do?"

I couldn't stand seeing her trapped like that. I stepped forward and tried to reach out to touch her.

"Don't!" cried Peter, when he saw what I was doing. But it was too late. I had already laid my hands against the blue light. I felt a tingle run through my body. For a terrible instant I thought I was going to be drawn into the force field, too. But it didn't happen.

What did happen was I heard a voice inside my head. *Susan, don't worry about me. You've got to warn the others!*

It was Ms. Schwartz.

"Peter!" I yelled. "Come here. Touch the force field. You can hear Ms. Schwartz!"

I suppose it sounded crazy. But by this time he was ready to believe anything. He pushed through the heavy air that surrounded the force field and put his hands next to mine on the column of light.

*Hello, Peter,* said Ms. Schwartz.

"Telepathy!" whispered Peter in awe. "These guys are amazing."

*Yes, they are,* said Ms. Schwartz inside our heads. *Amazing, and dangerous.*

"What do they want?" I asked.

*You!* she said.

I yelled and jumped back from the force field. The air around me felt so thick. It was hard to move through it. I realized I had lost my connection with Ms. Schwartz. Pushing forward, I pressed my hands back against the force field.

*I'm sorry,* said Ms. Schwartz. *I didn't mean to frighten you.*

I looked at her face. Her eyes were staring straight ahead. It was weird to hear her voice inside my head when she was standing there like that, looking as if she had been frozen.

*Don't worry about me,* she said. *Your job right now is to warn the others.*

"Warn them of what?" asked Peter.

*About Broxholm! His mission here is to find five students to take back with him. He plans to select the best, the worst, and the three most average kids.*

"What's he going to do with them?" I asked.

The voice inside my head sounded worried. *I don't know for sure. The plan is to bring them back here and head out into space on the night of May twenty-sixth.*

"But that's next week!" I cried.

Ms. Schwartz moaned. *I didn't know so much time had gone by,* she whispered inside our heads. *I can't keep track inside here. Listen, you have to unmask him somehow. If you don't, you're all in terrible danger.*

Just then we heard the front door open and close.

Talk about terrible danger.

Broxholm was back!

# CHAPTER TEN

# Solo Effort

My mouth went dry. My hands started shaking. Peter's eyes were so wide they looked like ping-pong balls.

*Shhh!* cautioned Ms. Schwartz. *Don't make a sound.*

I appreciated the advice, but I had already figured that much out on my own.

*What are we going to do?* I thought.

To my surprise, Ms. Schwartz answered me.

*Wait till he reports in,* she said. *Then you can sneak out.*

*Did you just read my mind?* I thought.

*Just the message you sent me,* she replied.

That was a relief! There's a lot going on inside my head that I don't want anyone to know about—not even Ms. Schwartz.

I looked around the attic. If Broxholm came up here we were sunk. I couldn't see a single thing to hide behind.

Suddenly I heard that horrible music again.

"This is our chance," I whispered. "He must be in his dressing room. I bet he's taking off his face and getting ready to report to the ship."

"Then let's go," said Peter.

"Wait," I said desperately. "What about Ms. Schwartz? We can't leave her here like this!"

*You have to,* she thought at us. *I'm all right for the time being. The best thing you can do for me is unmask the alien.*

I still hesitated.

*GO!* she shouted inside my head. The message was so powerful I staggered back from the force field.

Casting a last look over my shoulder, I took Peter's hand. He didn't pull away. This wasn't romance, it was terror. Each of us needed someone to hold on to as we sneaked down the stairway.

When we reached the bottom, Peter opened the door as quietly as he could. The tiny click was lost in the awful screech of the alien music. Moving slowly, he peered around the edge. "No one in sight," he whispered.

"Then let's go!"

My heart was pounding in my ears. I don't think I've ever been so frightened in my life. I had a feeling Broxholm would jump out and grab us at any second. For one horrible instant I wondered if the mirror on his dressing table might be at the right angle to show our reflections as we stepped out of the attic. I imagined him racing into the hallway, his Mr. Smith face hanging down around his chin, ready to turn us into a pair of puddles on the floor—or whatever a person from his planet did to kids he caught snooping in his attic.

The screeching music continued.

Still moving slowly, Peter closed the door behind us. That seemed like a waste of time, until I realized he was afraid that if he didn't secure it, the door might swing open after he let go of it.

One noise like that and we were dead meat.

Dropping to our hands and knees, we crawled along the edge of the wall. I couldn't help it—when I was opposite the door of Broxholm's room, I glanced in. Broxholm was sitting there, peeling off his face. I prayed that he wouldn't see me, and crept forward.

We slid down the stairs, slipped out the front door, and ran for all we were worth. After about three blocks we stopped to catch our breath. But not for long. In addition to everything else, I was worried that since Broxholm was back my parents might be home, too.

But when we reached my house I could see that I had made it back first. That wasn't too surprising. My folks often stayed to gab with the other parents after the formal meeting was over. It was even possible that the meeting was still going on, and Broxholm had managed to slip out early.

Peter walked me to my door. I thought that was brave of him—especially when I watched him walk off into the darkness and realized how frightened I would be if I had to go home alone. That skinny kid had more courage than anyone I knew.

As for me, I was terrified. I went around and turned on every light in the house. (Don't ask me what good I thought that would do. All I know is it made me *feel* better.) Then I sat in the living room, waiting for my parents to come home and worrying that Broxholm might show up first.

All in all, I decided it had been a good night's work. Even if I hadn't found anything to prove my story, at least one other person now knew what was going on. Even more important, we had found Ms. Schwartz.

But what should we do now?

The crucial thing was to reveal Broxholm for what he really was. But how could we do that without getting turned into puddles on the floor? Our only advantage was that he didn't know we knew his secret. If we could make whatever we did seem innocent, he might not guess what we were up to.

Of course, the most obvious thing was just to pull off his mask.

But how do you pull a mask off an alien's face?

I spent the whole night trying to find the courage to do what I knew I had to do the next day.

Mr. Bamwick had scheduled me for an extra lesson that morning. As usual, Smith/Broxholm shuddered when he saw me pick up my piccolo. Let him shudder! If he kidnapped me, maybe I'd play the piccolo all the way to the next galaxy.

The reason for the extra lesson was that Bam-Boom wanted me to work on a solo he had asked me to play for the spring concert. We were doing the greatest march of all time, "The Stars and Stripes Forever" by John Philip Sousa. (If you don't know it, you should go to your library and get a record of it so you can listen to it. It's great.) Anyway, the highpoint of the march is this incredibly neat, incredibly difficult piccolo solo.

Mr. Bamwick had told me way back in February that he had wanted our band to do this march for seven years. He said he had just been waiting until he had a piccolo player good enough to handle the solo, and now he thought he had one. Me.

I was flattered that he had so much faith in me. The problem was, *I* didn't have that much faith in me. Oh, I could do most of the solo right—most of the time. But there was one trill near the end that I always messed up. Let me tell you, if you're going to play something in concert you don't want to get it almost right. You want it perfect.

60

But Mr. Bamwick was determined we would play "The Stars and Stripes Forever" that spring, or die trying. The way my lesson was going that Friday, it looked as if we were going to die.

"Come on, Susan," said Mr. Bamwick after I messed up for the third time. "The concert is next week! Did you practice last night?"

I shook my head. "I didn't have time," I said.

I knew it sounded pretty lame. But how could I tell him I hadn't practiced because I had been prowling through my teacher's house, trying to find evidence to prove he was an alien?

I could see Mr. Bamwick trying to control himself. I have to give him credit. He knows that it doesn't do any good to make a kid feel stupid. But I could tell he really wanted to explode. By the time I left his room, I was pretty upset myself.

That wasn't *all* bad. Being angry gave me the strength to do what I knew I had to do. Taking a deep breath, I marched back to my room. I paused outside the door and took another deep breath.

Then I went through the door, staggered over to Mr. Smith's desk, and pretended to faint.

On the way down, I grabbed for his ear.

# CHAPTER ELEVEN

# Parent Conference

Failure! I had hoped to hit the floor with Mr. Smith's face in my hand and Broxholm's real mug exposed for all the world to see. Instead, I ended up with a handful of air and a bump on the head.

The other kids in the class shouted and jumped to their feet. Smith/Broxholm waved them away. He told Mike Foran to go get the nurse. Then he knelt over me to see if I was all right. He was acting so tender and concerned that I almost felt bad about trying to pull off his face. But all I had to do was think of Ms. Schwartz trapped in that force field in his attic, and any guilt I might have felt just floated right away.

"Susan! Susan, are you all right?" he asked, fanning my face.

I moaned and fluttered my eyes. "What—what happened?" I asked.

"You fainted," said Broxholm. He patted the side of his head. "Almost took my ear with you," he added. He gave me a cute little smile that showed the dimple in his right cheek.

Between the two of us, the air was thick with fake innocence. Was it really possible he didn't know what I was up to?

A minute later Mike came running back with Mrs. Glacka puffing along behind him. She checked my pulse, felt my forehead, and then helped me to her office to (surprise!) lie down.

She also decided to call my mother. This meant that I had to go home, and then to the doctor's, and then spend the rest of the afternoon in bed with my mother fussing and worrying about whether or not I was about to get my first period.

She even decided that I had to spend the evening in bed, too, after she brought my supper to my room.

"Gracious, Susan," she said when she burst through the door. "This place looks like an explosion at a garage sale. Can't you keep it a little neater?"

"I was planning to clean it today," I said. "Only I didn't feel up to it after I fainted."

"Poor baby," she said, setting the tray on my nightstand.

She seemed so pleased I decided not to tell her I had been kidding. She never could understand that I liked my room the way it was.

After supper I slipped out of bed and went to see my father.

He was sitting in his den, building a model of the Empire State Building out of toothpicks. That's his hobby—making famous buildings with toothpicks. If you ask me, it's pretty weird. But it keeps him happy, which is more than I can say for most adults I know. So I guess I shouldn't complain.

"Hi, Pook," he said when I walked in. "Feeling better?"

I nodded, not wanting to tell him I hadn't been feeling bad to begin with. I sat down next to him and started handing him toothpicks.

"So, what's on your pre-pubescent mind tonight?" he said, holding up a toothpick and dabbing a bit of glue onto the end of it.

"Dad!" I said. But that was all I could think of. I tried, but I just couldn't bring myself to explain the situation. After a full minute of silence he turned to me and said, "Are you all right, Susan?" I knew he was really concerned, because he let the glue on the end of his toothpick dry out while he was waiting for my answer.

"I'm fine," I said at last. "Well, not exactly fine. I've got a problem."

"What kind of problem?" he asked. He put down his toothpick and gave me his full attention.

This was terrible! Can you imagine trying to tell

your father that your teacher is an alien? He was going to think I was out of my mind.

But I had to do something. So I took a deep breath and said, "It's about Mr. Smith."

He nodded, inviting me to continue.

Look, I tried. I really did. But I just couldn't bring myself to say the words, "My teacher is an alien."

After a long, uncomfortable silence I finally said, "I don't think he likes me very much."

Dad looked appropriately worried. "Why not?" he asked.

"Well, he shudders whenever he sees me go to my music lesson." I hoped that might sound weird enough to get him to ask another question.

*Come on, Dad, help me!* I thought. *Ask the right questions.*

But he just laughed. "As long as Mr. Smith doesn't actually say anything, I don't think you can complain too much," he said. "Maybe the guy just doesn't like music. Not everyone can be as cultured as we are, you know. He's probably just a philistine."

*Yeah*, I thought, *A Philistine—from the planet Philis!*

But all I said aloud was, "Yeah. A philistine."

Figuring he had solved my problem, Dad turned back to his toothpicks. "I wouldn't let it get to you, honey," he said. "The school year's almost over. You can tough it out till then. Now, you better scoot back to bed before your mother catches you out here."

I gave him a hug and trudged back to my room.

Now what? If I was going to do anything about this mess, I had to get some proof, and fast.

I was still trying to figure that all out when Peter called.

"Nice try today," he said. "You're really brave. I just hope Broxholm didn't figure out what you were up to."

Great! That was the last thing in the world I wanted to think about.

"I wasn't brave," I said. "Just desperate. What I want to know is what are we going to do next? We've got to find some way to prove the truth about Broxholm."

"Actually, that's why I'm calling," said Peter. "I wanted to know if you had a camera."

"Sure. Why?"

He hesitated, then said, "Well, are you game for another expedition into Broxholm's lair?"

I smiled for the first time that day."So we can take a picture of Ms. Schwartz! Peter, you're brilliant. Only when can we be sure he won't be there?"

"How about during school?"

"Peter, I can't skip school! My mother would kill me!"

"Would you rather get kidnapped by aliens?" he asked

I sighed. "All right. I'll bring my camera to school on Monday. We'll talk about it then."

I hung up and tried not to think about the fact that in two days, I was going to go back into the alien's den.

In fact, I spent most of that whole long, sleepless night trying not to think about it.

# CHAPTER TWELVE

# Things Get Weirder

I didn't think it was all that weird when Stacy Benoit called me Saturday morning to see how I was doing. After all, she's my friend, and she did think I had fainted in school the day before. I didn't realize when I laughed and told her there wasn't anything wrong with me that I was only confirming her worst fears.

I didn't figure *that* out until Monday morning, when our class turned into something from the Twilight Zone.

Until that point, I had other things to worry about—like what to do about Ms. Schwartz.

Since my mother still wouldn't let me out of the house, I spent a long time discussing this force field thing with Peter over the phone. He told me he was pretty sure Ms. Schwartz was actually safer inside that thing than she would be walking the streets.

"She probably doesn't like it in there," he said. "I know I wouldn't. But nothing's going to hurt her."

"Well, doesn't she have to eat or go to the bathroom, or something?" I asked nervously.

I could almost see Peter's shrug over the telephone line. "I don't think so," he said. "I have a feeling time is pretty much holding still inside that thing. So unless she had to go to the bathroom when he put her in there, she's probably fine." He paused, then added, "Come to think of it, that force field could be a woman's dream—she won't age a bit!"

"Don't be a male chauvinist piglet," I said angrily. "This is serious."

"I know it's serious," snapped Peter. "But we can't do anything about it this weekend—unless you know of a time when we can be sure that Broxholm won't be there."

"I suppose you're right," I said.

But the thought of Ms. Schwartz trapped in that force field gnawed away at me for all the rest of the day and all of Sunday, too. I had to get her out of there!

I was still stewing about that on Monday, until things got so weird that I forgot about Ms. Schwartz for a while.

It started with Duncan Dougal, who walked into

class carrying the biggest apple I had ever seen in my life.

"Good morning, Mr. Smith," he said. "How are you today?" His voice was so syrupy-sweet it made me want to throw up.

I looked away, then looked back again so fast it put a crick in my neck. *Duncan?* I thought in astonishment.

The class bully put his apple on Mr. Smith's desk, then went to his own desk, sat down, and folded his hands neatly in front of him.

I squeezed my eyes shut and then opened them again to see if anything would change. But the apple was still there, and Duncan was still sitting at his desk, smiling like a little angel.

What was going on here?

When I opened my desk, I found a note that said,"I think you are the bravest person I have ever met." It was signed, "A friend."

Who had it come from? And why?

I looked around the room, but the others were all bent over their desks, working busily away.

I turned back to my work, trying to figure out what was going on. But even the weird stuff that had happened so far hadn't prepared me for what came next.

"You pig-faced baboon!" yelled a familiar voice.

Stacy? Stacy Benoit? The girl most likely to be declared a saint while still living?

I turned around and saw Stacy standing beside her desk, shouting at Mike Foran—the only kid I had ever heard of who had never, I mean NEVER, gotten in trouble with a teacher.

"Shut up!" yelled Mike. "Shut up, you creep!"

When Stacy slapped him across the face I almost fell out of my chair. Of course, Stacy couldn't slap that well, having never done it before. So it was kind of a wimpy little slap. But this was *Stacy Benoit*, for heaven's sakes.

"Stacy!" yelled Mr. Smith, who was sitting at the back of the room with a reading group. "Michael! What is going on up there?"

He started for the front of the room. But he was too late. When Stacy slapped Mike, he jumped up so fast he knocked his desk over. His face was red. I didn't realize until later it was from stage fright.

"You mother wears—uh, uh—your mother wears—"

I wanted to prompt him. It was pathetic to see the nicest kid in the class try to come up with a withering insult, and even more pathetic when he finally finished up with, "your mother wears polyester!"

But it seemed to do the trick. Stacy began to shriek in outrage.

Mr. Smith reached them just in time to keep them from going for each other's throats.

"The rest of you stay in your seats," he ordered. "I'll be back in a minute."

Then he walked out the door, dragging the two best-behaved kids in sixth grade along with him. They were kicking and screaming every step of the way.

I closed my eyes and shook my head. I was sure I was awake. So what was going on? Was this the same planet I had gone to sleep on?

I couldn't wait for recess so I could talk to Peter.

## CHAPTER THIRTEEN

# Rumors

"Stacy and Mike did a good job, didn't they?" said Peter, when we got together on the playground at recess.

"What are you talking about?" I asked.

"Stacy and Mike. Didn't you think that fight they put on was pretty good?"

"The fight they *put on?*" I echoed.

Peter sounded impatient. "Stacy and Mike are afraid Broxholm will decide one of them is the best kid in the class and then try to kidnap whichever one he chooses. So they decided to fake a fight— you know, mess up their reputations a little."

All of a sudden everything came clear. "*That's* why Duncan brought Mr. Smith an apple this morning!" I said.

Peter giggled. "Pathetic, isn't it? But it might work. Right now Duncan is a sure pick for worst kid in the class. But if he works really hard, he might actually manage to pull himself off the bottom of the list. Since he knows that no matter what he does, he's never going to push himself into the most average category, if he can improve at all, he's probably safe. The problem is, he's been so bad all year that it's going to take a major effort to get out of the bottom spot."

Peter paused, then added, "I intend to have some fun with him over the next three days."

Three days! That was all the time we had before Broxholm was scheduled to kidnap five of us into space.

"That's not very nice," I started to say.

But then I remembered the way Duncan had tormented Peter for the last six years. I decided I couldn't blame Peter if he wanted to get a little of his own back while he could. Any decision to be a nice guy about this was going to have to come from inside himself.

I decided to change the subject. "Tell me," I said. "Just how did they know about all this?"

"I told them," said Peter.

"And they believed you?"

Actually, it made sense. If they were going to believe anyone, it would be Peter. He had a reputation as being the most honest kid in the class, which was one of his problems. He didn't know how to tell the kind of "little white lies" that keep people from getting mad at you.

But I doubted that even his reputation for honesty would convince people this story was true.

Peter smiled. "Actually, you're the reason anyone believed me. It started with Stacy. She just didn't believe you had really fainted—or that if you had, you would have tried to grab the teacher's ear on the way down. So she knew something was going on. Later she cornered me on the playground and demanded to know what you were up to."

"Why you?" I asked.

Peter blushed. "You're going to hate this," he said. "There's a rumor going around that you're my girlfriend because we've been spending so much time talking on the playground."

"Yuck!" I yelled. "Yuck! Yuck! Yuck!"

Suddenly I realized what I had just done. "Don't take that personally," I said.

"I won't," said Peter. "Since I feel the same way."

*Hey!* I thought. *What do you mean, you feel the same way?*

But we didn't have time to work that out right then.

"Anyway," said Peter, "Stacy was convinced I must know what was going on. And since I did, I told her."

"The whole story?" I gasped.

Peter nodded. "She didn't believe me at first, of course. But when she talked to you on Saturday and you told her there was nothing actually wrong with you, she figured it must be true." He laughed. "That was all it took. By Saturday afternoon, the phone lines were humming all over Kennituck Falls."

"How come you know all this?" I asked. "How come no one asked me?"

Peter shrugged. "That's not the way rumors work. People never check with the source. They always ask someone else. Don't ask me why, but it's true. Lots of stupid things are true. Anyway, Stacy told Mike, and Mike told someone else, and that was it. It's the kind of story that travels fast."

"And they all believe it?" I asked.

Peter shook his head. "I don't think so—at least not yet. Except for Duncan. He's so dim he'll believe anything—especially if Stacy and Mike believe it. He thinks they know everything. That's why he hates them so much."

"I see," I said, though some of this was coming a little too fast for me. "Well, do you suppose if enough of us start to believe it, the adults will pay any attention to us?"

Peter looked as if I had just suggested Mickey Mouse was likely to be the next president of the United States. "Get real, Susan," he said. "They'll

say it's just another crazy kid rumor. Do you remember last year, when half the people in this
school were convinced that the president was
coming to Kennituck Falls to make a speech?"

I nodded. I had almost believed it myself—half
because so many of my friends did, half because I
wanted it to be true. I also remember how my father had laughed when he heard about it. "Just because a thousand idiots believe something, that
doesn't make it true," he had said.

Which was true, I guess. But it certainly didn't
help us now.

That was when Peter decided to complicate
things with a new problem.

"What are you going to do about this yourself?"
he asked.

"What do you mean?"

"Well, since one of the things on Broxholm's
shopping list is the best kid in the class, if we can't
unmask him you've got a good chance of being
picked yourself."

That was the best laugh I'd had in days. "You're
nuts," I said. "There's no way I could be picked
for top kid in the class!"

"There is too. It all depends on how he's making
his choice. The way I see it, there are four of us
that might be considered best in the class—Stacy,
Michael, you, and me."

"You're nuts," I said again.

"Listen to me! Stacy and Michael are your basic perfect students. But they just did a good job of taking themselves out of the running—though to tell you the truth, I don't think Broxholm would have chosen either of them, anyway. They're real bright, but they don't *think* that much. They believe everything the teacher tells them. I'm sure Broxholm is bright enough to know that doesn't make a great student."

He paused. "Then there's me," he said. "I'm real bright. But I'm not motivated. And I'm not very social. You know how it goes: 'Peter is a good student, but he's not very well rounded.' I hear it every year. That leaves you, Susan. You get good grades. You get along with everyone. You're in all kinds of activities. Let's face it, you may not be the best in any one thing, but when you look at everything together, you make a pretty good pick for top of the class."

I stared at him in horror. "You're not kidding, are you?"

He shook his head.

# CHAPTER FOURTEEN

# What Can
# Duncan Dougal Do?

I couldn't believe what I was hearing. I had been worried that Broxholm might want me for one of his "average" slots. It never even crossed my mind that I could be considered the top student in the class.

"Peter, what am I going to do?" I wailed.

Peter shrugged his skinny shoulders. "Don't worry," he said. "I've got a plan."

I thought he meant the camera. He didn't, but I didn't know that then. The plan he actually meant was so weird I never would have thought of it.

I took a deep breath and tried to settle down. "I'm glad you mentioned that," I said, referring to the camera. "I think I've figured out the best time for me to get back into Broxholm's house."

"You mean *us*," said Peter.

I shook my head. "I mean *me*," I said. "I'm going

to do it tomorrow morning, during my music lesson time. That way Mr. Smith won't suspect anything when I leave the room. I figure if I use my bike, I can make it to his house and back before I'm really missed. I'll get in trouble later, but at least I'll have the proof we need."

"You're not going alone," said Peter.

"Yes, I am," I said. "If we both take off, it's going to look suspicious—especially considering the amount of time we've spent together lately. Maybe suspicious enough that Broxholm will pretend he's sick, just so he can check up on us. We don't want him walking in on us while we're taking the photos. I doubt we could manage to sneak out of his house without getting caught a second time—especially if he's actually looking for us."

"Then I should go instead," said Peter. "You might not have enough time. I'll just skip school altogether."

"Now, how can you do that?" I asked.

Peter sighed. "I keep trying to tell you, it doesn't make any difference what I do. As long as I don't get in trouble with the law, no one cares."

"Peter, that's not a very nice way to talk about your parents," I said.

"I don't have parents," he snapped. "I've got *a* parent. Period. And he doesn't care what I do, as long as I don't get in trouble."

I felt stupid. Here I had known this kid for six years, and I didn't even know he only had one parent.

"All right," I said. "We'll go together."

"Why don't I just go alone?" said Peter.

I shook my head. "I got this whole thing started. It's my job."

Actually, I wasn't really feeling all that noble. I wanted to see Ms. Schwartz again—to make sure she was OK, and also to get some advice.

Peter shrugged. "You're the one who's going to land in hot water. If that's the way you want to do it, it's OK with me."

Then it was time to go back inside. Even though the major weirdness was over for the day, you could sense a kind of nervous energy in the classroom. The other kids didn't *really* believe the rumors about Mr. Smith being an alien—at least not yet. But after the little show Stacy and Mike had put on, they were starting to take things pretty seriously.

It would have been funny, if it wasn't so scary.

The next morning I rode my bike to school, carrying my piccolo and camera in my backpack. As I was putting the lock on my front wheel, Duncan Dougal came sidling up to me and said, "If you and Peter are pulling some kind of joke on me, I'm going to turn you into peanut butter."

Strange as it may seem, Duncan's threat made me feel better. At least I knew there were some things in the world that I could still count on.

"It's no joke, Duncan," I said, drawing a cross over my heart with my fingers.

He looked at me suspiciously. Then he nodded. "OK," he said. "Now, what are we going to do about it?"

Now that was something I *hadn't* expected: an offer of help from Duncan Dougal. *Think quick*, I told myself. *This may not happen again for another ten years.*

I looked at Duncan. "How would you feel about skipping school today?" I asked.

He grinned, showing the big gap between his front teeth. "I love skipping school," he said.

He wasn't telling me something I didn't know. One of the things that made it possible to survive having Duncan in our class was the fact that he was out of school so often. We all knew his older brother wrote his excuses for him. But none of us were about to tell; we weren't crazy enough to do something that would put Duncan in our classroom any more often than necessary.

Besides, if one of us told and Duncan found out who did it, he would massacre that person.

But it might be useful to have him along—if I could be sure of one other thing. "Can you go someplace with Peter without picking on him?" I asked.

"Sure," said Duncan. "I like Peter."

I looked at him. To my astonishment, he looked like he really meant it.

I shook my head. What can you say to someone like that?

"All right," I said. "You go do whatever it is you do when you skip school. I'm going to sneak out of the building at quarter after nine. I want you to meet me at the corner of Pine and Parker. You'll need a bike."

I thought about telling him not to steal it, but decided that might seem too insulting.

Duncan nodded his head. "Where are we going?" he asked.

I looked him right in the eye and said, "Peter and I are going to break into Mr. Smith's house and take pictures of the force field where he's holding Ms. Schwartz prisoner. I want you to stand outside and be our lookout, in case Mr. Smith gets wise and comes back to stop us."

I hesitated, then added, "I hope you won't mind facing an alien death ray."

I suppose that was a rotten thing to say. But the look on Duncan's face made it worth it.

## CHAPTER FIFTEEN

# Hookey for Three

I was so nervous that I didn't even look at Mr. Smith when it was time to leave for my lesson.

*Forgive me, Mr. Bamwick,* I thought as I headed away from his room, toward the side door.

Peeking out to make sure there was no one around, I sprinted to my bike, unlocked it, and headed out of the schoolyard as fast as I could.

Duncan was waiting at the corner of Pine and Parker, sitting on a blue five-speed.

"Follow me!" I said and kept riding for the edge of town.

I checked my watch. It had been twelve minutes since I left the class. If I could make it back just as fast, that would give me sixteen minutes to take the pictures.

Peter was waiting in front of the hedge at Broxholm's house. I could see his smile quickly turn to a frown when he saw who was with me. His pale face turned even paler as we drew up.

"What's *he* doing here?" demanded Peter.

I was impressed. It took a lot of nerve for Peter to say that in front of Duncan.

To my surprise, it was Duncan who tried to make peace. "I just came to help," he said. He did say it kind of belligerently, but he was holding up his hands with the palms out to show that he meant peace.

"He's going to be our lookout," I added, hoping that Peter would see the wisdom of this.

He hesitated for a moment, then nodded. "OK," he said grudgingly. "I guess you can stay."

Duncan looked as pleased as a naughty puppy who's just been let back into the house. "What do you want me to do?" he asked.

"Stand right here," I said, indicating a spot just inside the hedge where he could have a good view of the sidewalk. "If you see Mr. Smith coming, run up on the porch and pound on the door to give us a warning. Then run for your life!"

Duncan nodded seriously and took his place. I looked at Peter. He gave me a nod, and we headed for the back of the house.

To my relief, the broken lock was still where Peter had jammed it back in place after our last adventure here. I had figured that as a temporary tenant, Broxholm probably wouldn't keep that close an eye on things that needed repair around the place. It was nice to find out I had been right.

We opened the door, and headed back into the alien's lair.

I felt a little more at ease this time. After all, we could be pretty sure that Broxholm would stay at school. We knew exactly where we were going. And we had a lookout to keep us from being surprised.

How could we go wrong?

The answer to that question was even worse than I expected.

For the first few minutes everything went as smooth as could be. We made it out of the cellar and into the attic with time to spare.

Nothing had changed. The column of blue light was still there. And poor Ms. Schwartz was still trapped right in the middle of it.

I rushed over to it and placed my hands against the force field. Almost instantly I could hear Ms. Schwartz's voice in my head. *Hello, Susan. What are you doing here?*

*We came to take some pictures of you, so that we can prove what's going on,* I thought back at her.

Her reply scared me. *Weren't you just here a few minutes ago?* she asked. She sounded confused.

I bit my lip. Was she all right?

Of course, since the thought was about her, Ms. Schwartz picked it up.

*I'm not sure,* she responded. *It's getting so it's very hard to think in here.* She paused for a moment, then asked, *What day is this?*

*It's Tuesday,* I thought. *Tuesday, the twenty-fourth of May.*

Her reaction almost knocked me over. *You must do something!* she thought desperately. *It's only two days until Broxholm is planning his pickup. Susan, you have to do something!*

*I know, I know!* I replied. Her fear was coming through as clearly as her thoughts, and it was making me afraid, too.

Our conversation was interrupted by Peter. "Susan, we can't just stand here and chat. We've got to get these pictures taken!"

He was right of course. *Hang on, Ms. Schwartz,* I thought. *We'll get you out of there somehow!*

Peter had already started flashing.

"That's good," he said. "Let me get a couple more of you standing next to her. Then move away from the force field so I can get some of Ms. Schwartz by herself."

I was glad Peter was there. I might have gotten so wound up talking to Ms. Schwartz that I wouldn't have taken the pictures in time to get back to school. But he was working fast. In a few minutes he had used up most of the roll, taking some pictures with flashes, some without, working from all different angles. I helped, and we did everything we could think of to make sure we got at least one good shot.

We were just trying to figure out the last angle when we heard a terrible scream from downstairs.

"Ahhhhhh! Ahhhh ahhhhhh ahhhhh!"

I couldn't make much sense of the words. But I recognized the voice. It belonged to Duncan Dougal.

# CHAPTER SIXTEEN

# Duncan's Disaster

Peter looked at me. I looked at him. I wondered if he was as terrified as he looked. I wondered if I looked as terrified as I *felt*.

"What's *he* doing in here?" I whispered.

"And what's happening to him?" hissed Peter.

*And what are we going to do about it?* I thought.

We hesitated for only a second and then began to creep down the stairwell.

Duncan was still screaming.

We had left the door to the attic open, in case we needed to make a quick getaway. Poking my head around the edge, I looked in the direction of the screams. They were coming from the room where Mr. Smith sat to take off his mask every night.

I reached for Peter's hand. "What should we do?" I mouthed to him.

He pointed down the hall and started off with me following close behind.

After a couple of steps, we dropped to our bellies and slid up to the door and peeked around the edge.

I couldn't believe it—Duncan was all alone. He was standing in front of the "mirror," screaming for all he was worth.

I can't say that I blamed him—the communicator was on, and Duncan was looking into the bridge of Broxholm's starship. And one of those hideous aliens from the ship was looking back at him, talking to him in that language of growls and shrieks.

I took a deep breath and slithered into the room, crawling across the floor as fast as I could move. I scooted right under the table and hit the switch I had seen Broxholm use to turn the set off.

It made a crackling noise and then fell silent. Duncan stopped screaming.

"You idiot!" yelled Peter, jumping into the room. "What are you doing in here?"

"I got bored," sniveled Duncan.

Talk about a short attention span. He couldn't have been out there more than five or ten minutes.

"And I wanted to see if you were telling the truth or not," he continued. "So I went around the house and came in through the cellar. This was the only room with anything in it, so I came in. When I touched the switch, that—that—that *thing* showed up and started growling at me."

Duncan was blubbering now, with big tears cutting clean paths down his dirty face.

He turned to me and said, "Is that what Mr. Smith really looks like?"

I nodded my head.

Duncan's eyes rolled back in his head—and he fainted.

By the time we got him on his feet and out of the house, I only had ten minutes to get back to school.

"Maybe I shouldn't go back," I said.

Peter shook his head. "You have to," he said. "We can't afford to be more suspicious than we already are. Anyway, I don't think the aliens actually saw you—at least not your face. You stayed down low enough."

"What about me?" blubbered Duncan. "What about me?"

Peter hesitated. "You'll have to hide out at my house," he said. "It's the last place anyone would think to look for you. If you stay there, you *may* be safe. Get *going*, Susan; you've got to get back to school as soon as possible. Don't worry about the pictures; I'll take care of that. Just move!"

I hopped on my bike and headed for school. By riding extra hard I got there just about the time my lesson was supposed to be ending. But I was all hot and sweaty when I sneaked back in. Even worse, I ran into Mr. Bamwick the moment I walked through the door.

He was furious."Susan, where have you been?" he shouted. "I've spent the last forty minutes waiting for you. We've got a concert in two days, and my star soloist can't even show up for her lesson!"

I did the only thing I could think of: I started to cry. It wasn't hard to do, since I was on the edge of tears, anyway.

"I'm sorry, Mr. Bamwick," I sobbed. "I'm just so frightened I couldn't come to my lesson."

Wow! So far so good. I was actually managing to tell him something that was pretty close to the truth.

But then I felt bad, because Mr. Bamwick, who really is a good guy, got upset about scaring me and started apologizing for putting me under so much pressure.

In the end it worked out better than I could have imagined. Mr. Bamwick went to Mr. Smith and explained that there had been a problem with my lesson, and since we had this important concert coming up, would it be possible for him to keep me for a little while longer, and so on.

It was great! I had a real excuse, and I even got to work on my solo.

Back in class things were pretty quiet, until just

before the end of the day when Mike Foran started throwing spitballs at Stacy. I wondered if the two of them weren't actually enjoying themselves. After all, they had been so well behaved for the last several years that maybe this was the perfect chance for them to let off a little steam.

But it wasn't Stacy and Michael who were asked to stay after school that day.

No, that honor was reserved for yours truly. I was sitting at my desk, thinking that maybe we had actually gotten away with our litle photo session when Mr. Smith walked up to me and said, "Miss Simmons, I want you to stay after school. I need to talk to you."

It was amazing how two such simple sentences could teach me whole new levels of fear.

# CHAPTER SEVENTEEN

# Teacher Conference

The other kids had left. I was alone with the alien.

At least Stacy had lingered at the door for a few minutes—until Mr. Smith turned to her and said, "It's time for you to go, Miss Benoit. I want to speak to Miss Simmons in private."

Stacy looked at me with an expression that said, "I *tried*." Then she hurried away.

Broxholm/Smith walked over and straddled the chair in front of my desk. He leaned toward me. "I know what you did today," he said.

"Oh" was all I could manage. I felt as if someone had dropped an ice cube into my heart. The worst thing was, I couldn't even be sure what he meant. Did he know I had skipped my piccolo lesson? Or did he know I had been inside his house?

I looked at the door and wondered if I would ever go through it as a living person again.

"Well?" said Broxholm.

"I'm sorry," I whispered. It was about all my voice was good for at that point. It was also just as vague as his first statement. I wasn't about to say what I was sorry for.

Broxholm looked at me. "I don't understand why you dislike me so much, Susan," he said. "I'm just trying to do what is right for this class. Yet you've been hostile to me from the moment I walked through the door."

What an actor! I wondered if I would ever be that good. It was amazing how he was still pretending to be just a teacher who was having trouble with one of his students.

Suddenly he rose and crossed the room to close the door. "Now," he said, sitting down in front of me again, "let's be honest with each other, shall we, Miss Simmons?"

Should I say something? Should I tell him I knew his secret?

"Why are you here, anyway?" I said at last, still playing his game of not saying anything that couldn't be taken at least two ways.

"I'm here to learn," he said smoothly. "After all, isn't that what school is for?"

*Creep!* I thought. But out loud I said, "I thought you were supposed to be the teacher." I tried to keep my voice from cracking. But it did, anyway.

Broxholm shifted in his chair. "A good teacher is always learning," he said. "Education is a process of give and take. I have to *take* certain things in order to learn. Look at all I've taken from this class already. I've taken a lot of nonsense. I've taken a lot of snottiness."

Suddenly he turned and looked directly at me. "And I'll have to take a few *more* things in order to learn all I can—if you *take* my meaning, Miss Simmons."

I shrank back in terror.

I don't know how he did it, but I could actually see his alien eyes beneath his mask, as if they were burning with a light of their own.

"And I won't *take* kindly to any interference with my educational mission," he said in a voice without any emotion.

He had picked up a copy of *Rockets and Flags* as he talked. Now he began to squeeze it. I watched his fingers sink right into the cover, compressing the paper with the power of his grip.

I heard a horrible thumping sound. I glanced around to see where it was coming from, then realized it was the beating of my own heart.

"The universe is a very big place, Susan," said Broxholm gently.

He dropped the book. His fingers had left dents half an inch deep in the cover. If only I could get the book out of there, I would finally have proof of what he was. But, of course, he had no intention of letting me have the book. He picked it up and carried it to his briefcase.

"A very big place indeed," he said. "And there are more things going on in it than you can possibly imagine. It's important to learn all we can. Otherwise, terrible things can happen. Terrible things. That's my job—to prevent terrible things. Can you understand that, Miss Simmons?"

I shook my head. Maybe I should say I shook my head *harder*, since I was already shaking all over.

He sighed. "Well, perhaps someday you will," he said. "For now, I simply want you to know that it is wisest—and safest—not to interfere with your elders."

He closed his briefcase. "I will see you tomorrow, Miss Simmons," he said. "I trust that you will spend the entire day here in the classroom—and not enter my home again!"

I almost fell off my chair. He knew. He had known all along! Before I could say anything, he went out the door, leaving me alone.

## CHAPTER EIGHTEEN

# Concert Concerns

It took me almost twenty minutes to get home. I cycled along the sidewalk slowly, watching every corner. I kept expecting aliens to leap out of the bushes and grab me.

When something *did* jump out of the bushes, I screamed so high and so loud, I was surprised I didn't break the glass in the street lamp overhead.

But it was only Peter.

"Are you trying to give me a heart attack?" I asked, straddling my bike and glaring at him.

"It would serve you right for bringing Duncan along today," he said.

I wasn't up for a fight, and I said so. Peter was mad enough that he might have kept it going, anyway, but when I started to tell him what had happened after school he got so interested he forgot about being angry. He insisted that I try to remember every word Broxholm had said.

"Where's Duncan?" I asked when I finished my story.

"Hiding in my closet," said Peter with a wicked grin. "We called his folks, and he's going to spend the next couple of days at my house."

"Didn't they ask any questions?"

Peter laughed. "If you were Duncan's mother, wouldn't you be glad to have him out of the house for a while?"

I didn't think that was very nice, but I let it pass. "Will *you* be able to stand him till this is over?" I asked.

"My problem is trying not to take advantage of him," said Peter sadly. "It's not easy. I'd really love to get back at him for some of the things he's done to me. But he's so terrified I don't dare have any fun with him. I really think if I popped a bag near his ear he would have a heart attack and die."

I laughed in spite of myself.

"What about your father?" I asked.

Peter grimaced. "He won't even notice Duncan is there," he said. "By the way, I took the pictures to the drugstore. We can pick them up after school tomorrow."

"If we live that long," I said.

"Relax," said Peter. "Broxholm and his friends are here to collect people. I'd be really surprised if they actually kill anyone."

That made me feel a little better. But it was only the thought that this whole mess might be over when we got the pictures that kept me from losing my mind that night. Even so, I was so frazzled I couldn't think about anything else.

By morning I was such a wreck that my special session with Mr. Bamwick was a total disaster.

"No, no, no!" he kept yelling. "It's B flat, Susan. B *flat!*"

"Well, I can't get it right if you keep screaming at me," I said, trying not to cry.

I couldn't blame poor Mr. Bamwick. The concert was only a day away, and I was getting worse by the minute. But I just couldn't concentrate on the music. How could I, when I knew what else was supposed to happen? Could you play the piccolo, if you knew some of your friends—or maybe even you—were about to be kidnapped by aliens?

"Aren't you worried?" I asked Peter that afternoon on the playground.

"Not really," he said. His pale face split into a wide grin. "I told you, I've got an alternate plan."

"Listen, Peter," I said, taking his arm. "This isn't one of your science fiction books. And you're not Buck Rogers. Don't get carried away."

He shook my hand away angrily. "This is the greatest thing that's ever happened in this town," he said. "And don't you forget it, Susan!"

At that point Stacy and Mike went running by, yelling bad words at each other.

We started to laugh. "I heard Stacy say that her mother is going nuts," said Peter. "I bet Mike's mother is, too."

I nodded. I almost felt sorry for them. It can't be easy to have a kid who hasn't been in trouble since kindergarten suddenly turn into a maniac.

"Of course, Stacy and Mike don't have much choice," I said.

"Sure they do," said Peter.

"What do you mean by that?" I asked.

But he wouldn't answer me. "Just watch," he said. "You'll figure it out soon enough."

## CHAPTER NINETEEN

# Peter's Choice

That afternoon I finally began to understand Peter's "alternate plan."

Actually, it took me a little while to figure it out. I knew there was something strange going on when Peter—the kid who always knew the answer but never bothered to give it—started raising his hand for every question that came along.

And suddenly it all came clear to me. Peter *wanted* to be picked by Broxholm. He had decided that this was his big chance to live the kind of science fiction adventure he had been dreaming about. He figured if he really tried, he might just be able to make it from "bright, but unmotivated" to being, without question, the best student in the class.

You could almost see the gleam in Broxholm's alien eyes when Peter unleashed his mighty brain.

We were having a history lesson at the time, and Peter started to answer every question perfectly.

Broxholm started asking harder questions, but Peter never blinked; he just kept reeling off the answers. Even I had no idea how smart that kid was. (And as for Broxholm, I swear, that alien must have memorized an encyclopedia; or maybe he had one transplanted into his head. Who knows what these people could do?)

When school was over I dragged Peter off to the side of the playground. "Are you crazy?" I hissed. "What are you doing?"

"Plan B," said Peter. "If we can't unmask Broxholm, I want to be one of the ones to go on the ship."

"Forget Plan B!" I yelled. "You don't know what they're going to do to you up there. They're bad!"

"You don't know that," said Peter.

"They kidnapped Ms. Schwartz!"

He shrugged. "That still doesn't mean they're bad. They may be so far above us they think of us like we think of ants or something."

I didn't say a word. But he could tell by my expression that I thought that was stupid.

"Maybe they're scared of us," he continued.

That made me laugh.

"I'm serious," said Peter. "Think of that conversation you had with him yesterday."

"I can't," I said. "It still scares me."

"No, *think* about it," said Peter again. "Maybe these people are really peaceful. Maybe they've seen how much we fight, and they're afraid if we get much farther into space, we'll cause some huge war."

"You don't know that," I said stubbornly. "Anyway, maybe we won't have to worry about it. Let's go to the drugstore to get our pictures."

It took all our money for the pictures. I thought about explaining to the girl behind the counter that we were trying to stop an alien invasion, but I figured she probably wouldn't buy it.

We forced ourselves not to open the envelope until we were in the park.

"You open it," I said, handing the envelope to Peter.

He hesitated for a moment, then tore the envelope open and pulled out the pictures.

His face fell.

"What is it?" I asked.

Without saying a word, he handed me the photos.

My heart sank as I flipped through them. Peter had done a good job. The beams and timbers of the attic showed up perfectly. The focus and exposure were fine. But the force field with Ms. Schwartz in it had come out as nothing but a blue streak—

that was all, just a blue streak down the middle of each picture. It looked like a flaw in the film, or maybe some trick of the light. You couldn't see Ms. Schwartz at all.

"These aren't going to do us any good," I moaned.

Peter nodded. "I'm sorry," he said.

"It's not your fault," I replied. But I knew he didn't believe me.

By Thursday the whole school seemed to be on the brink of nervous breakdowns. Stacy got caught drawing dirty pictures on the blackboard. Mike tried out a new word he had learned from his uncle, who was a sailor. And Peter waved his hand like crazy every time Broxholm/Smith asked a question.

The ones who were really having a hard time were the kids in the middle. See, by this time, everyone was starting to believe the rumor about our teacher being an alien. I think the fact that Peter and I knew it was true, combined with the fact that we weren't *trying* to convince them was what really did convince them. They figured if it was a joke, we'd be trying to fool them. Since we weren't, it had to be for real. Or something like that.

Anyway, the kids in the middle were going nuts because they knew Broxholm wanted the three most average kids in the class. But what was an average kid? No one knew. So none of them knew how to behave to keep from being kidnapped. Most of them just acted the same as usual, except that they were really nervous. Every time one of them answered a question, you had the feeling they were trying to decide whether they should answer it right or wrong. It was like they were asking themselves: "Will a right answer get me a one-way trip in an alien spaceship?"

"I'll be glad when this is over," I said to Peter that afternoon during recess.

"Me too," he said. But I didn't like the kind of dreamy way he said it.

"Aren't you scared?" I demanded.

"I'm terrified," he said. "But that doesn't change my mind."

School just got wackier as the day went on. By the time the last bell rang I got the feeling every kid had heard there was supposed to be an alien invasion at the concert that night.

If I wasn't so worried, it would have been funny. "Did you hear about the invasion?" kids would say. "Did you know that the aliens are coming tonight?"

I wanted to say, "No, the aliens aren't invading. They're just coming to kidnap some of us." Although, for all I knew, the reason they wanted to study us was so that they could invade sometime in the future.

I felt sorriest for Mr. Bamwick. He had hoped to have the best spring concert ever. Now it was beginning to look as if it would be the biggest disaster of his career.

"I'm cutting 'The Stars and Stripes' from the program," he told me that afternoon. He was trying to be nice about it, but I could tell that he was really disappointed.

"I'm sorry," I said. "I just couldn't get that trill."

"No, it's not just you," said Mr. Bamwick sadly. "The whole band has fallen apart. I don't know what I've done wrong."

How could I tell him that he hadn't done anything wrong—that his concert was just another casualty of the alien invasion.

## CHAPTER TWENTY

# Piccolo Power

The alien-invasion rumors had reached the adults, too—as I found out that night at dinner.

"My goodness, Susan," said my mother as she was dishing up my broccoli. "I hope *you* don't believe any of this nonsense."

*Believe it?* I thought. *I started it!*

But I didn't say that. Instead, I put down my soup spoon and looked at her. "What if I did believe it?" I asked. I tried hard to sound like I was interested, not like I was challenging her.

"Well, I suppose we'd have to get you counseling," she said.

I could have cried. Obviously, there was no point in asking my parents to help out with this mess.

I went upstairs to get ready. *Which ones will it be?* I wondered as I slipped into my dress. *Just who is the alien going to steal?*

I looked in the mirror and crossed my fingers, praying that it wouldn't be me.

My parents drove me to the school. They dropped me off and went to find a parking place.

*I wonder how he's going to do it,* I thought as I walked through the door. *Will he just freeze everyone here on the spot? Will his ship use some sort of tractor beam to lift up his targets? Or will he wait until later, when everyone is asleep, and then sneak into their homes and snatch them?*

The school was fairly zinging with nervous energy. The rumors about the alien invasion had spread to all the grades. The third graders were walking around in pairs, checking over their shoulders every other step. If I hadn't been so scared myself, I would have laughed. I wanted to grab them and say, "Stop worrying. The alien's not after you."

"Hey, Susan," called Peter. "Wait up!"

Peter was in the chorus. The chorus was bigger than the band; almost every kid in the sixth grade was a member. They would be singing last of all.

Peter looked very nice. He had on a white shirt and a red tie. His pale blond hair was slicked down.

"Is your father here?" I asked.

He just stared at me. "Are you kidding?" he asked.

We walked on until we came to a private place. "What are we going to *do?*" I asked.

Peter shrugged. "What *can* we do? Keep our eyes open. Be ready to call for help when there's something we can prove. Other than that, I can't think of anything. Is Broxholm here?"

I nodded. All the teachers had to come to the concert to keep us under control while we were waiting to perform. I figured Broxholm wasn't ready to blow his cover yet.

Peter glanced at his watch. "We'd better get into the gym," he said. "No sense in getting in any more trouble than we have to."

The gym was where we had to wait for our turn to perform. It was across the hall from the combination cafeteria and auditorium where we put on our concerts. The third-grade chorus was about to go on when Peter and I walked in.

"Get over here, you two," hissed Miss Tompkins, the world's oldest living fifth grade teacher. "They're ready to start."

As we walked across the gym I heard the third-grade chorus begin to sing. They had only gotten through about three notes when the music stopped. I grabbed Peter's arm. Had it started?

Not actually; as it turned out, Cindy Farkis had fainted. The chorus teacher, Miss Binkin, stopped the program while two parents helped Cindy out. Then the singing began again.

"False alarm," said Peter with a grin.

I nodded. But I didn't feel like smiling.

Suddenly I heard a familiar voice. "Band members. Band members, over this way."

It was Mr. Smith. He was standing at the far end of the cafeteria, holding up his hand. "Band members, over here!" he shouted. "We're going down to the primary wing. Mr. Bamwick wants you to meet there to tune up."

"You can bet Broxholm won't stick around for that," said Peter. "Not the way he hates music."

Well, that gave me an idea. I might not have done it if I hadn't been feeling so crabby. But between the fact that we hadn't figured out any way to stop Broxholm from kidnapping some of our class and the fact that he was still holding the best teacher I had ever had prisoner, I was pretty mad. I decided if I couldn't beat the alien, I'd settle for annoying him.

So before we started down the hall I took my piccolo out of its case and put it together. Most of the other kids already had their instruments ready. Everybody was nervous. And it wasn't just pre-concert jitters. About half the band was made up of sixth graders. They were the *most* frightened, of course—especially the ones from our class.

"All right, follow me," said Broxholm as he started down the hall.

Holding my piccolo behind my back, I positioned myself at the front of the group. When we got about halfway down the hall, I started to play a scale.

"Stop that!" shouted Broxholm before I had played three notes.

"Just practicing," I said.

"Well, don't," he snapped.

I had never heard him sound so cranky before. I must have really gotten to him!

I began to wonder if I could break through his false front, get him to show himself for what he really was. I put the piccolo to my lips and began to play again.

"Miss Simmons, stop that!" he ordered again.

But this time I didn't stop.

"Please!" he said, clapping his hands over his ears. "Miss Simmons, please stop!"

I couldn't believe it. He was in agony.

I began to play louder.

"Susan," he howled, bending over. "Stop!"

I took the piccolo away from my lips for just an instant. "Not on your life—*Broxholm!*"

Then I started to play again, the best piccolo music I knew—the solo from "The Stars and Stripes Forever."

"Stop it!" shouted Broxholm, stumbling down the hall ahead of me. "Stop, stop, stop!"

"Help me, you guys!" I said. That was a big mistake. As soon as I took a pause from playing Broxholm spun around and snatched at my piccolo. But I pulled it back to safety before he could tear it from my hands.

"Take this, you alien creep!" I cried. And then I trilled him with a high C.

He backed away, holding his hands to his ears.

I went back to "The Stars and Stripes," starting at the beginning. I heard Mike Foran join me on his saxophone. Then Billy Gootch brought in the trumpet. We advanced on Broxholm, playing for all we were worth. He retreated down the hall, his handsome face twisted with pain.

Now the clarinets were coming in. And the rest of the trumpets. Then came the drums. And finally, deep and low and powerful, the sousaphone.

We sounded fantastic.

Mr. Bamwick came running out of the room where he had been waiting for us. "They're playing it!" he cried in joy. "They're playing it!"

But now I heard Dr. Bleekman charging down the hall behind us. "What's going on out here?" he roared. "Smith! Bamwick! Can't you keep those kids under control?"

"They're playing it!" cried Mr. Bamwick joyfully. "Seven years I've been waiting for this."

"Stop that!" roared Bleekman.

"No!" cried Mr. Bamwick. "Don't stop now! Let me hear it!"

We couldn't stop. We were on a roll. We had never sounded so good. And Broxholm was crumbling before us. "Stop," he pleaded. "Stop, stop!"

Adults were crowding out of the auditorium and into the hall. "What's going on?" they shouted. "What's happening out here?"

We reached the big finale. I played that trill like I had never played it before. We kept advancing on Broxholm. Soon the new Kennituck Falls Elementary School Marching Band had the alien cowering in a corner.

"What do you want?" he pleaded.

I didn't dare stop playing. I knew my piccolo was keeping him at bay. But Mike stepped in. "Take off your mask!" he shouted.

"Your mask!" cried the others. "Take off your mask!"

"Anything!" said Broxholm. "Just stop that noise."

"First your mask!" cried the band.

Even Dr. Bleekman could see that there was something weird about his favorite teacner now.

He waited in silence.

I played my trill again.

Broxholm reached behind his head, and began to peel off his face. Behind us people started to scream. Someone cried "What is it? What's happening?"

"Oh, my God!" yelled someone else. "It's Mr. Smith—he's—he's—an *alien!*"

# CHAPTER TWENTY-ONE

# Out of This World

I thought it was over. But I was wrong. Broxholm was still crouched against the wall, about two feet from the doors to the outside. The rest of us were about ten feet away from him, staring in horror at his strange alien features.

Suddenly the door to the left of Broxholm opened. It was Peter. He must have run out the front doors and circled around.

"Broxholm," he shouted. "This way. Run!"

The alien jumped to his feet and took off as if he had rocket-powered roller skates. As soon as he was through the door, Peter slammed it shut.

The rest of us started to run, too. Then Broxholm pulled something that looked like a thick pencil out of his pocket. He pointed it at the doors and fried them shut.

I started to tremble. He could have pointed that thing at me if he had really wanted to! He probably could have melted my piccolo to my lips.

*Maybe old Broxholm wasn't so bad after all*, I thought as I stood with my face pressed against the window, watching the alien and my best friend disappear into the night.

*My best friend?* I thought in surprise. But I knew it was true. Peter *was* my best friend.

And now he was gone.

Someone had called the police. Pretty soon their cruisers came screeching into the school yard. My mother was flapping her hands and worrying that I might have some alien disease.

With all the yelling and shouting, it took the police a while to figure things out. But soon they put me in a patrol car and we hightailed it out to Broxholm's place.

We were only a block from his house, when we heard a roar, followed by a high whine. Then this thing—this beautiful huge silvery sphere with a wheel of lights spinning around it—lifted into the air ahead of us.

"Stop the car," I said.

I don't know why, but they did—probably because the ship was so amazing. I pushed my way past the policeman on my right and stood in the road, watching the ship rise on a column of purple light into the black night. "Goodbye, Peter," I whispered. "Have a good trip!"

I felt as if something hard had become stuck in

my throat as I watched the ship soar higher and higher, until it was lost among the twinkling of the stars.

The police sealed off the house, just in case there were any aliens left inside. When they finally decided it was safe, I took them to see where Ms. Schwartz had been held prisoner.

I was afraid Broxholm might have taken her along. But when we climbed up into the attic, we found her sitting on the floor saying, "This is the worst headache I have *ever* had!"

"Ms. Schwartz!" I cried. I ran to her. She held out her arms and I fell into them. The two of us cried for a long time, which I think kind of confused the policemen.

The rest of the house was empty, except for a note from Peter we found stuck to the refrigerator door. He asked us not to worry and said that he would probably come back again someday.

And that was that. Things are back to normal now—at least, as normal as they ever get around here. Duncan has been picking on everyone he can. Mike and Stacy have regained their angelic reputations. (Though to tell you the truth, I wouldn't be surprised if they decide to get into a little mischief now and then just for the fun of it.)

As for me, I'm doing fine—except when I play my piccolo. That's when I think of Peter.

Sometimes I go outside at night to look at the stars. I try not to think about how far away Peter is. I only remember how much he wanted to go there. I do wonder where he is and if he's seeing all the wonderful things he used to imagine when he was reading those crazy science fiction novels.

Of course, I never *really* wish I had gone with him. After all, I've got a family that loves me. I like my life here on Earth.

But I wonder, sometimes, what it would be like to travel the stars with aliens.

Or maybe with *earthlings*. I've been studying my math pretty hard lately. I've kind of changed my mind about being an actress. I'm thinking maybe I'll be a scientist when I grow up.

I'd like to invent a ship—a ship that would take us right out of the solar system—out to explore all those distant stars that fill the sky at night.

Worlds where *we* would be the mysterious aliens.

Wouldn't that be something?